All he wanted
was a
Holiday

I

I initially found diaries a frivolous addition to one's livelihood - after all, an artist will inevitably fail to live in the moment if his head is forever lost in a book; hands preoccupied with autobiographical narcissism. At present however, one finds it necessary. Every hour spent in this foreign country must be documented to maximise poetic inspiration for it is, after all, my reason for travel.

I don't recall the last time I did such - It has been many years since I journeyed to Vienna, it must be, for I recall I honeymooned with Isabelle. O' it troubles me to remember that woman - so full of life yet untimely taken - alas, the mystery woes me to this day and plagues my nightly thoughts with ghastly images that I pray shall cease with time. A wicked adjudicator indeed - two years married to my Catherine yet like clockwork I wake each night to the same, horrific nightmare. Perhaps, a change of scene will warrant greater clarity of thought. This entry shan't be thus polluted with mournful rambles for one is all too aware of how it grieves my dear Kitty. I should hate to see her worried - one mustn't let on to the full extent of my troubles, nor, indeed, allow her pure heart to be weighted with such.

I must note this longevity is greater than any previous time spent apart; one cannot help but feel my reason for such abrupt departure was that of selfish nature - but for her sake, and our marriage, I must find means of income - impossible in London with the dammed black cloud of grief that e're blots my creative sun; ink shall flow here, I am sure. My talent shall finally prove pragmatic in this tight-fisted society.

Her adopted Father - stern, army man - never approved of my profession; said it unbecoming and emasculating of a traditional Gentlemen. I believe these accusations false, but I am yet to oppose such a rank as Captain! Alack, for I recall his mantle exhibits an Enfield from the Crimea... Nay, one mustn't convey such unjust malice - wildly protective of my Catherine is he; such that could only be interpreted as wanting the best for her. As do I, of course, thus in recent years we have reached a comforting understanding.

I must opine therefore that equal to his stern exterior is the possession of a good heart yet, sadly, such that was never reciprocated by a woman - even before the demise of Catherine's parents I never recall his mention of female company. Indeed, one is inclined to believe him invariably career-minded and so disinterested in matters of the heart. My wife informs me I needn't threat as to his solidarity; the Captain has recently befriended one Mr Butcher - curious man, equally infatuated by the likes of militaristic pastimes and recreation in the wilderness. Queer indeed! I belive it Shakespeare who stated 'faithful friends are hard to find' - I am certain therefore of his remaining in fair spirits whilst I am away on business. Perhaps us gentlemen shall share our respective adventures over dinner upon my return; I'm faithfully informed my Father-in-law's new acquaintance possesses ample culinary skills.

Note: *Personal* - This reminds me of British food. I must enquire as to what my accommodation serves as I fear my palate may disagree with Eastern foods as per my... *grievance...* in Venice.

Just as I am comforted by The Captain's kindness; I feel equally reassured that throughout my Journey Catherine will remain in good morale whilst I am away and In the protective company of two respectable gentlemen. I had hoped her company would expand to peers - perhaps the opportunity for ladylike pastimes or a visit to those quaint little cafés she enjoys for afternoon tea. But, alas, I fear such is simply impossible since her dear friend Alison was taken ill. A most peculiar case; so much so that one feels rather improper disclosing it within these informal pages - but I feel it best to pen one's thoughts rather than share qualms with my troubled wife.

Aye, it has been almost three months since she was taken into the care of one Dr Micheal Cooper - a sudden turn that not even Catherine had reasons to suspect! An exchange of letters informs us she has since reduced to feminine hysteria; crippled by violent hallucinations that e're persist both day and night. Dr Cooper marks thus an inexplicable ailment as she is supposedly convinced as to their truth - the contents unchanging as if her madness holds eerie consistency. Her reports tell of a 'grey lady' that warns of impending disaster; she talks of fictitious beings set to destroy London with queer rituals and decadence! O', how the fair Lady hath fallen! I think it best her Asylum is overseas (closer to I than Catherine) as I fear seeing her friend in such a state shall cause unnecessary upset.

I was at first sceptical of Dr Cooper's specialisation in holistic medicine (such modern cures as hypnosis and herbal remedies) but I now acknowledge an unorthodox case is cause for unorthodox solutions! I am confident therefore of Alison's best care - and pray for Kitty's sake for her swift and absolute recovery.

Nay! Enough with such dross! I fear I should bring the woe away with me and henceforth pollute such a beautiful country! Indeed, Catherine should love it here, I believe. At present the evening's dusk illuminates the eastern landscape with such exquisiteness - almost supernaturally so. I long to compare my wife to the beauteous likes of the scenery I have witnessed thus far; vexed only the carriage windows obscure my view. Perhaps I am at fault for seeking refuge in such an isolated area - indeed, I feel as though the road is e're inclining! I profoundly hope the quality of my living arrangements justify the route's longevity.

Such a journey, I find, inevitably warrants fear of postal delays as should I write to Catherine (as I'm assured she to me) one cannot help but question the timing - at present I feel this country rather backward in comparison to home if letter delivery should be anything like travel; my dear shall be waiting a while for my word!

The people too have proven relatively hostile - nay, hostile is perhaps too strong - but alas the local's appear to have rashly established some vendetta against my foreign-ness. I do believe it the language barrier that prevents further communication; what I've witnessed thus far warrants the justification that perhaps this is for the better:

I was approached by a young woman mere hours ago before the coach arrived; unkept brown hair and a strong jaw. She wore surprisingly fine clothes; queer, for a lady of her status - but as were her words, lord! She informs me of her missing Husband - recons it the works of those who reside in the very house I am staying at! I must heed her warning, says she, and avoid the mansion at all costs (or something similar, regrettably her French accent was rather hard to decider alongside the broken English.)

It would be false to say this encounter hadn't unnerved me slightly; but I think it merely an attempt to deter me from their country. My driver appears content and, as he resides there, I am more inclined to think his truth. The travel agent deemed it cheap accommodation, but nothing out of ordinary was reported. No rituals of supernatural sort as she suggests; nor religious curiosities (I believe this area incredibly superstitious) - not that I could see regardless! The heavens seem e're blotted by a ghastly fog. There is an undoubtable atmosphere to this area - alas, I fear it a mixture of fatigue and the trick of the setting sun - but at certain angles I swear my driver's head intermittently disappears. Such terrible falseness! I must rest before these visions worsen... I mustn't let her words dissuade me from logical conclusions.

Later:

It had long since surpassed nightfall when the driver pulled up to the house - he and I had been heartily conversing as to it's history. A strange fellow - somewhat enigmatic despite his being English but O' such charming wit and Humour! I recall him turning to me upon a particularly narrow path:

'Don't look down' said he; gesturing to the rocky precipice below.

'Indeed, quite the fall!' I reply 'does it not unnerve you to manoeuvre such a perilous route?'

'It is not often I have to' he replies ' we don't get many guests these days.'

I thought this interesting, and so continued my investigation - perhaps such insider tales should spark ideas.

'Oh? Pray tell, is there a reason I should know?'

'Nothing sinister' he assures me with a chuckle 'people just prefer guesthouses that ain't in the middle of nowhere.'

I laugh 'I see! I do hope there is activity to keep me from solidarity?'

'It's a beautiful house, sir' he tells me 'great big library that should keep a type like yourself entertained.'

'And the guests?' I enquire 'am I to have company?'

'Not at present' the driver sighs 'did have a mrs - Lady - Button staying but she was taken ill' quite some time ago. If you don't mind me saying Sir, bit ov' an old Hag; good to see her go!'

I laugh; inexplicably infatuated by the man's company 'Indeed my late mother was similar - never believed in my work - vexed me greatly! But Catherine tells me I shouldn't speak such malice.'

'That's woman for you' he snickers 'invariably meek, I do envy their temperament! Who's Catherine, Sir? That your girl?'

'My wife' I correct with pride; thankfully he sees such as lighthearted 'I shall miss her whilst away on business - but I assume you face similar with your work? You are married, are you not?'

I watch his face fall, and thus I fear I've put my foot in it quite profoundly. I recall scrambling for forgiveness; backtracking all the whilst spouting dross until he finally says:

'Sophie. That's my girl. Haven't-' he clears his throat 'haven't spoken to her in a while is all.'

'I apologise.'

'Ay, no time to dwell on it' I am delighted by a small smile which tugs at my forgiveness 'we're here.'

Certain as his words we pull up to a immense building that seemingly materialised from nowhere. It's harsh, antiquated features like cragged spires amongst the e're thickening fog. It would be false to claim my person did not succumb to a shiver. The driver takes my coat and bag as I exit the coach.

'I never got you're name' I subtly enquire as we walk with trepidation to the door.

'Mr Bone, Sir' he tells me with a crude little wink 'but you can call me Humphrey.'

The building itself is quite astounding; decoration the likes of which I have never witnessed back at home. The design reminds me of those gothic builds one reads about in novels or the travel section in the local gazette - perhaps one day I shall have my piece published there! Although there is little to describe at present due to the darkness - the house is not yet subject to electric lights. An archaic overhead lantern instead illuminates the threshold; a dark, thick wooden door with what appears to be bolts across the middle. On the front; a large brass knocker in desperate need of oiling.

I hadn't the chance to take my hand from the metal before the door is swung open by a curious gentleman; short, unshaven and scantily-clad in a hastily-fastened burgundy dressing gown. Humphrey appeared unfazed by his appearance; thus I take it upon myself to grow accustomed to what I assume is simply more cultural differentiation. If somewhat idiosyncratic; the man appeared friendly - glancing up at me with remarkably blue eyes; wide and inquisitive.

'Thomas' says he with an unplaceable accent 'Thomas Thorne?'

'I am he, Sir.'

'Please' the gentleman grinned 'call me Robin.'

Perhaps this sounds silly; but the connotations to such a British bird grants me an inexplicable sense of comfort. I know not where he acquired such, perhaps his family have traveled in history. I thought it best not to pry at present - focused more on the interior of the luxurious house I now found myself in. Humphrey takes my bags upstairs whilst 'Robin' invites me to the drawing room.

His hair is somewhat matted, I note (he also he appears to be wearing woman's stockings... but I've no doubt this is another custom; either way I'm certain this man shall be the subject of many limericks to come) and fingers adorned with jewels. I believe this man very wealthy indeed - if I were perhaps more shallow; I may even dismiss these oddities as eccentricity. I note too that his lips bear a red stain almost identical to lipstick.

'Is it customary to wear makeup?' I tentatively enquire 'your mouth.'

To this he licks his lips, just so that he bears some of the sharpest teeth I've ever seen! White and bestial all the whilst a long, serpentine tongue dances playfully across his mouth.

'probably blood' he chuckles rather macabrely.

'I beg your pardon, Sir?'

'We have steak earlier' he informs me, 'like it... *raw.*'

Once again the scenery prevents further enquiry as I am brought into yet another room. It appears more quaint than the hallway; less marble and lavish decor make for a comforting change to the ostentatious front. The drawing room possesses familiarity to my own in London; a fireplace and armchairs accompanied by a bookshelf and brandy cabinet - from which Robin produces a glass and fills it generously.

'You're kind sir' I tell him 'but I mustn't stay long - you must understand I've had a rather long journey.'

'Sure, sure' he nods 'sit now; can go when want.'

His broken English amuses me as I do as he instructs - taking the glass and sipping gently. I do embarrass myself as I recoil at it's strength!

'Good, eh?' He laughed - I'd like to believe I mustered a nod between coughs.

The light of the fire warrants better view of his features - youthful; I note - there's a playfulness threatened by lines that crease his eyes; still e're mesmerising. He bears those unnerving teeth with every smile. We talk for sometime about his country; the house - I tell of my life and profession to which I believe he approves; he fancies himself to be better aquatinted with English literature.

'I believe you said 'we' earlier' I finally recall 'pray, Humphrey said there were no other guests?'

'Non' specifically' he responds in a gravelly tone 'we all eat together here - staff like family to me.'

I thought this most unusual, but decide against further enquiry.

'Mary to thank for food' he continued 'she in room couple' doors down from you - probably catch her at some point for breakfast, eh?'

'Indeed Sir, I shall.'

'Oh! And Julie opposite you - that pretty much it for people.'

'Julie?' I repeat 'is she a maid?'

He emits a raspy laugh '*he* just a… *friend…* name actually Julian - Julie little nickname because, in many ways, he girl - specially' when we…'

Vexingly, he does not finish his sentence - merely looks to me with a devilish smirk as if I should understand. I can only assume this 'Julian' is some sort-of effeminate tennis player.

'I see' I lie, glancing to the clock (of which has long since struck midnight) 'I suppose I should be getting to bed.'

Robin gets up for a reason I still fail to decipher. He places a hand on my shoulder; giggling clumsily whilst his fingers snake around my cravat.

'Gotta watch what you sais' in this house' he informs me with a smirk 'someone might take that as an invitation.'

I laugh to ease the tension, shaking his hand from my person (he's joking, surely) 'perhaps I should stress *alone*?'

'Clever boy' he grins; watching me go with a rather sadistic smile that unnerves me momentarily.

There is no lock to my door; one of the only doors without one it appears! I mustn't dwell on it now. My room is splendidly lavish - I've no doubt I shall sleep handsomely and begin my work refreshed tomorrow.

II

Anxiously awaiting my husband's word I busied myself with baking today - yet not even apple pie has proved sufficient in calming my nerves! I shouldn't like my husband to worry himself whilst on holiday and so in vain I've tried to be patient... and not sit by the door for *too* long awaiting the post.

I shall miss my dear Thomas; although excited by his journey I am most disappointed we shall spend such time apart. As a poet; his letters are always so wonderfully descriptive... so I suppose his beautiful words will transport me there with him. Oh, I do long for his word! What if he's unwell? Or unhappy? No, he is surely fine. I am to blame for jinxing such with awful thoughts.

My Father comes in two days with his new acquaintance; I'm certain such lovely company shall distract me from my troubles. I hope to visit town and catch a picture; and after perhaps tea and cake! It shall be most exciting to see him again. I had rather hoped to arrange such with Alison too; but I can merely await her recovery. Oh, God bless the lovely Doctor Cooper for sending me regular letters to ease my anxiousness. I wait for his word often too.

Alas, waiting appears all I ever do around here - one cannot help but find it awfully dull! I must find excitement in the little things to avoid boredom; perhaps set myself tasks to feel accomplished. Yes. I have decided. Today was baking - tomorrow shall be picking an outfit for Father's visit. I've a lovely purple dress that Thomas and I purchased in town before his departure that he's yet to see. I do believe it will more than suffice for our day out.

Indeed, memories of Thomas sometimes cause upset - but I can banish such unhappiness when I think of him happy; surrounded by wonderful landscapes and scenery that I'm sure will inspire equally beautiful poetry that he'll read to me on his return. The thought of such keeps me in high spirits - I've many questions to ask in letters! How was his Journey? What is his accommodation like? I'm certain he will meet many interesting individuals on his travels...

Thomas Thorne's Diary, 22nd September.

Alas, I know not whom to offer my forgiveness for not writing; but in all honesty I have spent the day exploring my residence. One cannot comprehend the size from the outside; every hallway like extensive catacombs that I shall surely get lost time and time again - the present darkness provides no aid to my situation. Ay, catacombs with nothing but dead ends, it seems, for every door appears locked and bolted. There are many floors to the house too... although I am yet to venture past the second as I fear I shall be greeted with yet another maze of corridors!

I have little to note of the day - perhaps it is because I didn't rise until midday (sleep hindered by some insatiable groaning... I do hope this shan't be a reoccurring disturbance.) I was rather hoping to explore the village but, in hindsight, I think it best the day's events panned out as such - today has proven immensely valuable in getting my bearings (after all... I should hardly expect to walk the town if unable to locate the dining room!)

Speaking of such; what I have found thus far is most peculiar. The room itself is, like everything in this house, remarkably lavish and extravagant - the table could easily seat twenty. The kitchen however is horridly bear and seemingly abandoned - as though the residents have never cooked or e're stepped foot in it! This oddity makes the immaculate silverware and goblets look a touch performative. I can only assume there are other facilities for culinary purposes that I am yet to find.

Regardless; I managed to put together a substantial meal from the provisions in my suitcase (I have packed more than enough to last, one can never be too careful in my unfavourable circumstances) - I shall have to enquire later this evening when one should expect dinner. It should be nice to converse as I haven't seen a soul all day! Perhaps they have other business I am at present unaware of.

Later: In vain I searched the house for them as the evening drew near but I was unsuccessful. Disgruntled; I pause to rest on a chaise longe - red and velvet - that I find in yet another hallway. The moment I sit down however I am affrighted by a pair of eyes that I notice to the right of me. They are green, luminous; like that of a wild animal watching their prey from the darkness.

'…Hello?' I call with trepidation 'is someone there?'

The figure, now established to be a tall gentlemen, steps out of the shadows. He's slender and pale; almost extraordinarily so, and his hair blonde and rather unruly. Like most members of this house I find, his modesty comes in short supply with an unbuttoned shirt, blood-red and thin silk - trousers black like his thick leather boots. The man flashes me a smile that yields the power to both interest and unnerve me as he makes a (curiously) sultry walk toward me.

'I don't believe we've met' says he, looking me up and down 'and you are…?'

'Thomas' I answer 'Thomas Thorne. I arrived last night.'

'Ah, the poet' he exclaims - English too, I note - 'aye, Robin said you'd be coming.'

As the man steps closer; my eyes involuntary trail down to his bare chest. I cannot help but notice the bruises that litter it; curious wounds that appear red and raw - as though he'd suffered some recent affliction.

'Are your alright, Sir?' I gently enquire 'your… chest…'

'oh? These? He pulls the shirt to reveal more before I cast my eyes to the floor 'nothing to worry about. I've had worse.'

'I see' (in matter of fact I see far too much.)

'I'm Julian,' says he with a nod 'pretty sure you've heard of me.'

'Indeed Sir, I have' I hold my hand out to shake; but curiosity he takes it in his own - a touch so tender and forwardly intimate as he kisses it - as though I his Lady. Perplexed, I offer a smile in aid of appeasing his customs (I've no doubt I too shall learn these foreign oddities during my stay.)

'Mind if I join you?' He asks; I grant the affirmative before he sits by my side.

'It should be nice to get to know my housemates' I opine 'are you staying long?'

'Happen I am-' he laughs 'I do live here, Thorne.'

'Apologies. Robin did inform me.'

'No matter,' he places an icy hand on my shoulder 'permanence does lend to boredom, you understand. It should indeed be nice to talk to a new recruit; a little tête-à-tête.'

I don't dwell on the term 'recruit' nearly as much as the last phrase. I fancy this man may be similarly well traveled.

'Ah, French' I seed with a nod 'Have you been?'

'Learned it at school' he corrects 'you and I can appreciate written knowledge, I'm sure.'

'Indeed, Julian' I find his present company most refreshing - who were to guess that such distant lands could possess such like-minded individuals.

'Came from Cambridge, before I moved here' he tells me 'spent many years acquiring knowledge of the world. You could even say I'm... *well learned*... in certain practices.'

Perhaps I misunderstood, for when I ask if he's similarly well read he laughs - with such volume in fact I believe his outburst caught me off guard quite significantly.

'Not a literature scholar like yourself,' I'm informed 'more interested in the... *anatomical* side.'

'A Biologist, Julian?'

'Aye, studied the residents here most *intimately.*'

'*All*?' I weakly enquire, so ill at ease I mustn't have noticed the man shuffle closer to my person 'even-?'

'Especially' he interrupts 'and sometimes the three of us together. Been that way for a while - Robin recons it should be nice to have some... fresh blood... as the expression goes.'

And I should've seen it then. O' villain villain smiling dammed villain! I gulp as he leaned inchmeal forward.

'So; am I right to conclude t-that the two of you-' I believe I stuttered this enquiry; I was after all hideously out of my depth 'have... *together*...'

'Many times in many ways Thorne,' he grins; flashing those ghastly teeth that bear the mark of decadence 'does that repulse you? *Thrill* you? Tell me, what make you of this?

'Sir-I,' he looks over my person as I find myself instinctively cowering backwards - pinned against the chaise lounge like a green girl on her wedding night! Lord, I know not what possessed me but, nay, in that moment I found myself inexplicably paralysed. Transfixed; delirious - positively hypnotised by those exotic green eyes that e're inch closer to my face. Alas, it pains me to even pen such an intimate encounter but, should Catherine read this atrocity- heaven forbid! I must justify the hierarchy - one cannot help but yield to submission when challenged by such sensual power.

'I know not what to think,' I finally try - 'really-'

'Then don't,' he tells me; fingers, slender like a woman yet his touch bore no allusion the introversion of femininity as they brush across my chest 'let that brilliant mind stop churning for once, Thorne. Books don't teach you how to *feel* - isn't it within you to acquire a better understanding? Let me teach you, Thomas.'

'I am *married* sir' I attempt, his expression remains unchanged 'married two years to-' my words are cut off by a torturous finger to my lips.

'Ay and chastity tells unsatisfactorily so' he breaths, dammed lips brushing the pulsing veins of my neck as my arms instinctively push at the body that threatens to drown me in sin. In that moment I feel powerless, frighteningly so; yet some absurd curiosity prevents further intervention.

'You're mistaken-'

'Chastity of pleasure' he corrects, in a tone so bestial his diction is almost sacrificed to a growl 'one can be *intimate* without *intimacy*, Thomas. Let me teach you the ways of pleasure. Don't you yearn for better understanding? Be my Eve, take the apple.'

And then our mouths hurriedly meet. Speared teeth tear through my lips as blood seeps between us, polluting my mouth with the bitter taste of transgression as we groan - he of pleasure and I of pain. I hadn't the clarity of thought to ponder his perverted allegory (something of seed consumption or juices I darn't dwell on). Instead I pull away, appalled by the bloody lips that now taunt me, pigmented by my own affliction. I promptly wipe the abysmal redness that drips from my own mouth - staining my white sleeve in the process which, vexingly, grants this wanton imp further pleasure. It was as though he were aroused by the inadvertent symbolism of impurity.

'Why stop at red?' He tells me; straddled just so that I can feel his shameless interest; hands searching for my own that I've thus far denied him 'You've granted me a taste Thorne, don't deny me more-'

'I shall!' The beast hisses in anger as I strike those iniquitous hands away 'We mustn't- think of propriety, morals!

'Oh but we must!' He echoes as if to mock me. I am truly captivated; yielding unwillingly to the cold hand that snakes around my throat. His touch is maddening, yet something a libertine part of me craves. I can only believe it bewilderment that paralysed me; tranquillising my better judgment in the midst of this hasty escalation.

'What's morality's place in a dark empty room?' He continued, breath harsh and commanding against my ear 'what to propriety when secluded from all that is civil? You're in our land, Thomas; beset by decadence.'

'I am beset with *duality* Sir!'

He grins; I believe myself transfixed by his gaze 'take off the armour of convention. I should love to see your helmet.'

'Nay, never!' I blush, unwillingly producing some obscene groan I didn't know myself capable of as bloodstained lips kiss my neck; impish fingers toying with the fabric of my shirt 'think of Robin! Shouldn't he mind?!'

'I fancy he shouldn't' the horrid thing chuckles 'quite the opposite-'

'Good god he'd enjoy it?!'

'Aye, Thorne-' oh lord his hand trails down, *down* 'best put on a show- I'll have you practiced enough to join the ranks; you'd love it all of us together-'

'I shall do no such thing!' In vain I struggle gainst' a hold that should surley subdue Houdini! Vice-like claws clasp my wrists with inhuman strength.

'Oh come now Thomas,' he kisses my neck 'won't you reconsider?'

I open my mouth yet alas I'm betrayed by silent prose as the man lifts his head to look at me. I meet his gaze - eyes like emerald spirals e're spinning, glistening with such beauty I found myself unable to look away. Submission sets through my person as the need to struggle inexplicable disappears. Again he bore those pearly daggers; but I find myself smiling back - I am lethargic; horridly giddy to the point of drunken delusion.

'Oh, *Julian*' I gasp - these words are not my own! 'perhaps…
I *shall…*'

I have no memory of what happened next bar some terrible hiss of pain - we break eye contact and I find myself… *myself* again. A figure at the door phases into view, blurry; but I can make out the silhouette with what appears to be a crucifix in hand. Julian recoils, seemingly repelled by this ecclesiastical artefact.

'Go on, off!' The figure yells, wielding the symbol like some great weapon 'get away from him!'

'Know your place-' Julian growls, backing himself against a wall 'this doesn't concern you-'

'Nor should it Thomas!' he responds; and with a final affront from religion the perpetrator mutters some curse in Latin I, regrettably, haven't the means to translate - '*hoc non est finis*' - before disappearing back into the shadows.

With heartwarming immediacy, my saviour is then by my side. The man sits me up; his face finally visible as he glances over me with concern.

'Thomas?'

'Humphrey?' I slur 'is that-'

'Ay, are you hurt? Did he-'

'Nay nothing. But what in *God's* name was-'

'Come,' he tells me sternly 'we've much to talk about.'

III

It would be some terrible falsehood to pen that I'd planned a seamless deliverance. The rescue of Thomas was solely down to the fortune that I should be walking past - and having to hand the means for success! Call it luck; I care not - but only a fool would refuse to act after being granted such a golden opportunity. If one were to believe in fate; I do believe God has granted a blessed example.

Naturally; the man was frightened after the ordeal. I recall after the check of injury I asked him to follow me.

'But how should I trust you?' Said he with spite 'how am I to know you won't act as *he* did? I know nothing of this house! This could be some horrid conspiracy against me! You work for him, do you not?

His scepticism was understandable; but regrettably I hadn't the time for empathy. With a firm look of honesty I pull at my lips, revealing my teeth and true intent.

'I am not like them' I say 'in vain they try - which is why we must act *now* Thomas. We've little time; I ask you *please* to trust me.'

'Trust you?' Says he 'Sir, how could I *possibly-*'

'Be it them or I?' I pose - to which he falls silent in contemplation 'well?'

Wordlessly he stands; my offer had evidently proved sufficient. Perhaps not in gaining his trust, but it were enough for him to follow.

In little time we arrive in my room - I watch the man marvel (I think in hindsight his expression was more perturbed) at the copious documents that carpet my bedroom floor. I forget sometimes such extensive research is unconventional - to an outsider unaware of it's importance it must indeed make for quite the spectacle! Perhaps to him I appear some conspiracy-driven madman.

'Goodness Humphrey' he picks a book from my desk 'what *is* all this?'

'Research' I tell him blankly 'I think it wise to know of the threat we face.'

'What we *face* Sir is men whom haven't the-'

'No, no!' I dismiss his close-mindedness with an exasperated sigh 'you think too rationally, Thomas. These beings cannot be categorised with logic - for their existence poses no compliance with such. We face a threat far greater than human comprehension; which is why thus far they've been able to continue unopposed!'

'Sir you talk as though these people are otherworldly! What, pray, *is* this supernatural threat?'

'Vampires, Thomas!' He folds his arms at my sincerity 'I do not lie, Sir!'

'Humphrey, this is utter lunacy!' The man throws his hands dramatically 'these scriptures hold nothing but the rambles of madmen and conspirators! I cannot believe you'd subject me to the falsehood of mythical creatures and expect me to- you're unwell, Sir. I do believe this isolation has-'

'Indeed, Thomas' I refrain my anger in aid of proving my sanity 'I'm quite well. And quite correct. If logic be the object of your scepticism let me provide you with evidence-'

'Really, Sir-'

'Do they walk by day or night?'

'Well-'

'Aye! And you're intimately acquainted with their sharp teeth, unconventional ways - what to the kitchen, ay? E're seen you any food?'

'I thought that just-'

I tire of his excuses and thus I push him to sit. With haste I pull at my collar to reveal the affliction that has been wearing me down for weeks. He gasps; recoiling at the very sight of those abysmal puncture wounds which finalised my case. The man shivers; not from the gore but from the profundity of realisation.

'Good God-'

'Ahh, now you see it!' I believe myself then quite manically triumphant 'these wounds mark their horrid bite - drained of blood and energy Thomas, in vain they try to turn me but I'm yet to transgress by drinking their own!'

'What a sadistic ritual-'

'Aye, and this is just the start!' I pace the length of my room as Thomas e're turns whiter 'from the moment I heard of this supernatural cult I invested all my interest in stopping it. Took this job as a coach driver to acquire inside knowledge of their true intent-'

'That being-'

'Travel!'

'Travel?' He repeats.

'Aye, but not without soil, Thomas!' I hand him the manuscripts that told me such 'one of their queer limitations - that and ecclesiastical artefacts- vampires cannot relocate without the earth of their homeland.'

'But surely' the man pauses 'surely one can easily acquire-'

'In theory aye, but legend tells of a vampire long ago thwarted by that very over-confidence. They have the intelligence not to risk history's repetition.'

'Then how-'

'They talk of an ancient burial ground - home to ancestors; one of the few with stones still intact. If blood should meet the soil on full moon they are therefore forever bound to sacred earth; then to London they are permitted to travel.'

'Where *is* this land?' He asks; clasping his hands in aid of concealing his uneasiness 'and why to London?'

'Is it not obvious? To expand their race!' I reply; in hindsight perhaps to aggressively (his ignorance shouldn't anger me) 'once in the Capital they plot to corrupt the citizens to a villainous society of decadence and primordial urges; destroy life as we know it Thomas!'

'Good God Humphrey-' he stands before sitting again 'full moon you say? But that's-'

'Less than a week, aye-'

'But if you knew then why-' he rises again to pace the room 'why haven't you escaped? Told someone this- how do we *stop* this?!'

'Thomas, Thomas!' I place my hands firmly on his shoulders 'even if the doors weren't bolted I'd get nowhere - I've not the strength to travel on my own-'

'To f-find help; you could-'

'Who'd believe me, Thomas?' I shake my head 'you yourself could scarcely comprehend what you've witnessed first hand!'

'Surely Sir, we must *try*?'

I crack a smile at his earnestly; to which he cocks his head in understandable perplexity.

'You're willing?' I ask.

'Of course, anything.'

'There's a way out' I explain 'a window on the third floor that opens just enough to climb down the terrace-'

'Insanity!' Says he with a gasp 'Humphrey that's-'

'Our only option-' I finish 'unless one opts for the bloody alternative.'

'Dammit *both* these are bloody alternatives!' He shakes his head, exhaling in aid of collecting himself 'and should we survive; to where shall we go?'

'*When* we survive; we'll to the Button inn. It's not far and we should be safe until one can gather reinforcements.'

'Shouldn't they find us at such close proximity?'

'Happen they shouldn't' I opine 'for that's the last place they'd expect us to be.'

He considers 'reinforcements you say? Pray, know you of anyone?'

'Regrettably not. I'm yet to contact Sophie. Per chance do you-'

'I've contacts' says he with a nod 'I shall send a telegram upon our arrival.'

'Then it's decided. They sleep by day. Soon as dawn breaks; we flee-'

'So soon?' He gasps; the veil again stripping him of comfort 'but Humphrey-'

'We pose as a threat to the operation, Thomas' I say, hand on his trembling shoulder 'we'll soon be eradicated if we don't act *now* -'

He gulps, pale and affrighted 'e-eradicated?'

'Aye, I'm all to intimate with the consequences of their... last... vendetta.'

'Oh good heavens-' the poet stagers backward as I sit him in my chair 'good God what *have* I gotten myself-'

'Daren't dwell on it Thorne we've no time for madness!'

He composes himself; exhaling with pained longevity 'I apologise sir- you must understand this-'

He doesn't finish his sentence; but I believe myself acquainted well enough with his thoughts. In so little time I've broken this man's perception of reality; warped the realms of believably yet expect him to follow me unquestionably - to devise a plan with a straight mind no less! The tole that weights on out success however makes no room for sympathy. I can only hope one day, when this ghastly ordeal is over, I shall have his forgiveness.

'I understand Thomas. But you *must* trust me. There's too much that depends on it -far greater than you or I.'

'Sir-'

'Thomas' I say 'do you want to live?'

'*Heavens*, Humphrey!'

I look at him sternly 'live for your Lady?'

'Of course! Good God why ask such- '

'Then it's decided. To the Inn at Dawn.'

Julian Fawcett's Journal, 23rd September. ~6:38 AM.

Entries appear few and far between in this dammed book. I don't write - what's the need? These unimportant pages are to be penned and never viewed again.
In situations such as these however I feel documentation is *perhaps* in order.

Regrettably; it took me many hours before I'd the state of mind to find Robin - more than likely it being nearly sunrise that persuaded my judgment. This occurrence must be shared sooner rather than later after all.

I was not afraid; it can be categorically stated I felt no fear approaching our bedroom door. I know my darling should give me no reason to feel such. I can however disclose my… *minor*… qualms about disclosing such significant failure.
Not my fault, mind. I had him! Had him right where I wanted and dammit that - one cannot comprehend the frustration that comes with submitting to the power of a blasted piece of wood! How and where that bastard acquired it I'm practically insensible. All I know is this complicates matters greatly; and the Poet most certainly *isn't* on our side.

Outside the door I exhale; somewhat unwilling to break the news as I inevitably feel partly responsible for the loss. Despite the threshold unnerving me I enter with a smile. A problem shared is a problem halved (I believe someone said) - with a matter this pressing it's a damn good job one can thrice divide it!
With confidence, therefore, I enter my own damn room - relieved to find my lover in bed; holding our Lady to his chest - of whom smiles upon my arrival.

'Julian!' says she, 'you've been gone near' the whole night! Whats you been doing?'

'Heh' Robin grunts with a devilish smirk in my direction 'more like *who* he been doin', eh?'

'Oh' Mary suppresses a chuckle through her fingers 'aye.'

It is then that the man walks toward my person; a mere once-over with his eyes that yields the power (even after all these years) to make me shiver quite tremendously.

'Think Julie found a new playmate' his gravelly tones harsh against my ear 'What's he like? He ready to join us now? Bet he is with *you* doing the persuading-'

'Robin-' In vain I attempt a response but ,regrettably, his hands grasp my concentration '*Christ*-'

'Lets him speak love' Mary says; she presses a kiss to his cheek as he obeys 'if that be the case he probably spent like anything!'

'That it, ay?' I watch my lover's face fall as I assume mine did too '…Julian, What the matter?'

'That *bastard's* got a crucifix!' I blurt from seemingly nowhere. I still regret such an unchecked outburst - I must've looked a right bloody fool.

'Who has?' Mary's eyes widen 'The Poet?'

'No, *Humphrey*-' Robin paces the room as I continue 'I had him -well, had him with hypnosis- then he emerged from god-knows-where and yields the damn thing like a weapon! He knows - but *how*? How did he find out we can't-'

'Folklore, there's books abouts our type' Mary says 'but how'd he get it? There's nought in the library. Burned em' when we first moved in! We don't let him out to-'

'That what he want us to think-' Robin growls 'he been doing research. Argh! Should've turned him when I had the chance-'

'No, no this is my fault-' I say, eyes to the floor in aid of concealing my shame 'I sparked the- I'll talk to-'

'No time,' says Mary sternly 'near' sunrise now.'

Sure as her word the sun threatens to surpass the horizon as we turn our attention to the window - but that isn't the only grievance that those panes reveal. Just beyond the courtyard I watch two figures climb the gate; bags in hand as they rush away with telling urgency.

My eyes widen 'that's never-'

'...Aye' the other observers say in unison.

'I'll after them' I offer without thinking 'we've time before-'

'No!' I'm then slammed with unapologetic brutality against the harsh, stone wall - wincing as Robin balls his fists around my shirt 'what the matter with you?! You got death wish, eh?!'

I stutter the negative - the exactness of my denial I can't recall but it were enough for his expression of rage to diminish at the sight of my fear. He exhales, eyes conveying an earnest apology as he releases his hold; defeated.

'Won't risk it' says he, turning away '... can't lose you, Julian. Not for *anything.*'

And I do believe it then that his fondness broke me. Whilst I wish I could've seen his expression; I am grateful we neither of us bore witness to each other's emotion - for I fear I should never recover from such tenderness. Wordlessly therefore; I place a hand on his shoulder.

'I'm sorry' I say in all honesty 'Robin I-'

'Is not your fault' he tells me with a quiet smile. I believe his truth.

'Truth it be' Mary opines 'you weren't to know.'

'Way me see it; man with cross headin' in opposite direction, eh? Can't hurt us no more.'

'But what if he gets others to?' I say clutching his sleeve 'he's convinced the Poet, who else dammit?!'

'Shh, Julian' his kiss is effective in doing such; brief yet insistent 'who believe some madman who show up outta' nowhere?'

To illustrate his point; Robin waves his arms rather comically. Mary and I laugh at his spectacle.

'Oh, help me!' Says he in a most amusing tone 'vampires try take over! They come to London and fuck everyone!'

'See, is ludicrous' Mary chuckles 'there's nought that'll believe them.'

'Exactly' Robin nods 'time before ritual next week. We get on with that; no problem. They irrelevant to big picture.'

'Aye; we mustn't dwell on grievance and let it become distraction.'

'If you're sure?'

'Quite' says he 'now; to bed.'

Telegram: Thomas Thorne to Catherine Thorne. 23rd September.

My dear. I mustn't pen detail that shall worry you - but I must urge thee to obey these instructions with immediate effect. You shall meet me, my love, at the Button inn (The address is disclosed below) and there I shall reveal all. Know you this - I am safe. I am at present well. You mustn't let secrecy panic you. We simply cannot afford it.

Until we meet again. I love you; and I apologise for such cryptic prose.

IV

It would be grotesquely inappropriate to conclude that luck plays any part in such horrid circumstances; but I must opine that I feel both relief (and upset) that my Father's visit should occur on a day that warrants the need for great support - he has never failed to provide me with such, bless his heart.

In all honesty was beside myself with worry upon my Husband's mysterious word; I haven't the nerve to express further commentary bar my immediate preparations for departure. Indeed; one could argue the idiocy of conforming to such vague instruction; but I beg you to understand the delicate precariousness surrounding my husband's word is something my loving judgment cannot afford to dismiss. For now; there is hope -with regret nothing more. I cannot conceal my worry; but I know not what else there is to be done bar follow his word verbatim. He is my love, after all. My very oath of marriage vows to trust and support him regardless of how unorthodox his requests are.

My Thomas, although an emotional man, knows of my own nerve - I believe therefore his reason to conceal context is, although vexing, invariably for my protection. He would never exaggerate what is expected of me; regardless of my feminine qualms I must banish all for clarity of mind as he says. I must therefore facade bravery until we meet, content in the knowledge he would trust me with such a pressing matter - well, I assume - O' great heavens! I do believe it impossible to *entirely* rid entirely of doubt; his assurance of health could be but a white lie amidst his senseless rambles - perhaps the two interplay? My dear has gone mad and like Alison ill at ease in foreign lands! '*We*' says he; whom?! Thomas may be alone with his thoughts, in danger - good God let it not be so! I cannot bear the thought of such; my emotions beg I place down this trembling pen and compose myself.

Later:

I do acknowledge the irony of my outbursts as, indeed, they greatly distract me from rational judgment and, therefore, action. I realise now thinking so pessimistically shan't amount to anything bar my own unhappiness.

Yes, Catherine, you must remain positive - lord knows Thomas depends on it. I believe gathering my things before Father arrives shall distract me; although God knows *how* I will explain such an impromptu departure! The poor dear, I'd never even thought of such! I cannot simply-oh, no! I should look so terribly rude rushing around; but one simply mustn't abandon urgency for curtesy sake; he shall understand. God! How many times have I wished such? My Father deserves more than the shiftings and evasions of his selfish, *selfish* Daughter! And his companion, great heavens, what a simply awful first impression I shall make! When he arrives, I shall tell the truth and nothing but. It is then up to him what he makes of the Thorne lunacy.

Captain——'s Journal 23rd September.

Indeed, tonight's entry reads like some great work of dramatic fiction. Eighteen hundred hours ~~give or take, regrettably I left my watch at the house~~ Patrick and I arrived at my Daughter's home.
I had been greatly looking forward to visiting, admittedly I believe it Kitty who would benefit more from the company given her husband's recent excursion; but I safely pen that mutual relief should come from seeing her. I do believe ~~Pat~~ Patrick too remains in pleasant anticipation ~~It shall be nice for the two I love to get to know each-other~~ I've no doubt they'll get on.

Curiously, upon entry, the door was swung wide open. Catherine's safety seemingly unlocked and breached.

"You'd have thought she was expecting us" Patrick chuckled, signalling for me to lead our entry.

"Indeed" I nod, admittedly too perplexed to acknowledge his jest "best foot forward."

Upon arrival; Patrick and I are forced to step over dresses and possessions that litter the floor most untidily! I believe I shook my head; Catherine really should keep the house tidier - even in her husband's absence. This, I thought, was most unlike her; so much so that I began to feel ~~terribly worried~~ marginally concerned as to the effects of this isolation.

"Catherine?" I call with trepidation "what on earth is all- where *are* you?"

And then the madness unfolds, good lord! Almost instantaneously my Kitty comes rushing down the stairs in a most unladylike manner! Her beautiful complexion paled something horrid; great, hastily-fastened suitcases in either hand with an expression of profound hysteria.

"Oh, oh Father! Mr Butcher!" She flashes us each in turn a manic smile "you're- You're early!"

"Quite on time, actually" says Patrick, perplexed "aren't we, Cap?"

"Yes-I-" I look past her cheerful facade; eyeing her with paternal concern "Kitty, what *is* all this- are you-?"

I am not permitted to finish my enquiry as my Daughter promptly drops her bags. She launches herself onto me in a childlike embrace; clinging to my person as though I should disappear at any moment. I clear my throat; glancing to Patrick whom takes off his hat with an expression of astonishment. E're cheerful is that man yet I can tell Kitty's upset pains him as much as I.

"Dear Kitty-" I pat her back with caution "are you-"

Regrettably I make nothing from her muffled sobs, therefore I clasp her shoulders and hold her firmly in front of me as I did when she was younger.

"Come come" I say "this will never do, will it? What on *earth* is the matter? "

"Oh, Father I-" she sniffs, an abashed hand covering her mouth "I must compose myself. Excuse me, gentlemen."

My companion and I watch as she takes a seat in the drawing room, inviting us to do the same. She clutches a crumpled handkerchief - such I can tell has been used liberally this afternoon. The dear girl exhales; looking to us both with misty eyes.

"I must apologise to you both" she says finally "this is not at *all* how I wished to greet you."

"Please don't fret Catherine" - a genuine smile of assurance from Patrick - "something upsetting you?"

Kitty weakly nods; we look to each other knowingly as she produces a piece of familiar beige paper. Wordlessly, she hands it to me.

"I've received the most troubling news" she shakes her head as I read the cryptic telegram "I do believe Thomas is in some sort of danger."

"Good Lord-" (I believe I muttered) "…danger?"

My eyes scan the paper e're faster as dread sets in through my person. Patrick reads with equal haste over my shoulder. I hear mutters; he straightens his glasses with that familiar look of seriousness.

"I don't understand it" he says to Kitty "this is *all* you received, Mrs Thorne? Nothing more informative? Nothing at all?"

"You've read every word. Dear God I know not what to make of it!"

"In vain madam I've tried" says he "but-"

Their words trail off. Perhaps it the army strategies fronting; but already I feel my formulaic mind churning with pragmatic approach. My poor Daughter's frailty and nerve has most likely prevented her from achieving the same. Paper in hand I rise with purpose; my comrades looking upon me expectedly.

"We've no time to waste!" I say "my bags, Patrick! We'll all to the Button inn."

"Father! Good heavens!"

"Captain-" Patrick rises with alarm "you can't be- your not suggesting, Sir, that we peruse this- this wild goose chase with nowt but-"

"This is a call for help, Patrick! We cannot sit idly by in the knowing possession of such a mysterious SOS! In good conscience I will not leave Catherine in any more distress or uncertainty. I-What kind of soldier would I be if I left a man behind!?"

And there it is; that damned smile that I find a pleasant rarity amongst his other expressions. His glance is knowing, perhaps loving, but that simple look conveys his trust with a prominent glint of admiration. I believe Kitty saw it too, but did not understand its profundity in the same way as I.

"You're sure?"

"As certain as Death; A message like this cannot be ignored Sir."

"No, pray no talk of death, ~~Theodore~~ Captain" he gesticulates to my troubled Daughter, in hindsight perhaps the morbid expression was in poor taste "I'll to the house for travel papers and supplies. I think it best you stay here and comfort the poor pet."

Kitty finally stands "I beg you stay one moment, Sir! I don't think it practical not to *talk* before-"

"We've nothing to discuss" I assert "Catherine, this telegram holds no substance to do so! Don't you agree time is critical in such unorthodox circumstances?"

"Father; this is wholly impractical!"

"Were it not you running around with baggage?"

"…Yes Sir."

****

Patrick takes our carriage home; I note Kitty's uneasiness as he pulls away.

"Oh, such *haste*" says she "Father, I do not think I can take such frantic-"

"'*With immediate effect*'" I quote from Thomas' telegram "are those not your husband's words?"

"Well, Yes. And I must obey, I know! But Father everything has- it's all gone so bad so terribly quickly! And with equal haste you find yourself and your friend caught up in this madness! And, lord, you *believe* his senseless rambles too!"

"Of course Kitty, heavens, were you to believe otherwise?" I shake my head "you are my *Daughter*; he is like a *son* to me! I'd be a foolish man not to act upon your Husband's plea."

She grants me a small smile "perhaps, we are both fools for believing this madness."

"King Lear teaches that the fool makes for a persistent companion" I reply "Witty, loyal, and tells truth of everything. If Thomas is alone in that damned land I think it quite lucky we his fools."

"Oh, but Father-" she turns away "how terribly needy I must appear to ask for your assistance like this! I shouldn't ask so much of you. Indeed, perhaps I should travel alone-"

"Now that *is* truly foolish" I fold my arms "For a man to request assistance from his wife; then the matter must be most desperate. What Father would I be to let my vulnerable daughter travel alone?"

"You're too kind" says she with a smile "and Patrick too! Lord, I am eternally grateful for-"

"You're ahead of yourself" I try a laugh "we haven't saved him yet."

Pat's Journal 23rd September.

I do believe these entries would've been largely the same should I have written daily - an express train window view making us all terribly anxious - so, instead, I choose to write today as we near our destination. The train is to arrive tomorrow; then we've only a short carriage journey to the inn. I find this terrifically relieving as, indeed, the monotonous blur of the outside does little to settle my nervous stomach - but, god! What a woman I'd look to complain when poor Catherine has thus far facaded indifference; she's being so terribly brave for her husband's sake and, I note, her Father's too.

I know the Captain worries - as do I, of course, we've comitted to a blind battle and know nowt of the opposition, or even what bloody fight we face! It would be a lie to say the uneasiness of a military man does not distress me. Perhaps it because his Daughter is involved, but I have never seen the man quite like it in all time I've known him…

Across the carriage he mindlessly watches the scenery; I've no doubt his head is full to the brim with paternal concern.
We're *all* out of our depth here, I needn't be surprised we none of us know what to do with ourselves until we're united with Kitty's Husband. Poor lad, I do hope we're able to help. I'd hate to return to London defeated after all this elaborate scheming.

I would've thought my detachment from the family would've made this easier, but I can't deny sentiment has taken its tole on my indifference - as though I've become a part of this clan's queer ordeals. In the short time of my involvement I feel positively submerged in it! Regardless, to help the Captain would be a great honour and, if all's well, it'll be a lovely holiday. I should be able to sample some local delicacies, perhaps take some recipes back to London…

Kitty's Diary, 28th September.

The carriage journey to the Button Inn was *terribly* tense - I do fear the long travel has lessened our respective moral. Every day that passes without Thomas I grow increasingly unsettled - I pray each night for his safety and that we aren't too late. My Father and Patrick have been nothing but support to me, their assurance has been simply wonderful. That being said, I cannot help but notice my Father's concern - I do hope this prolonged suspense isn't too much for his poor heart. I sometimes wish I'd have never involved him.

The country is lovely; just like I expected. The sun sets beautifully over the landscape and the valleys make for a wonderful contrast to urban London. In vain I try to appreciate the beauty; but I admit I can hardly find anything exciting whilst my Husband's situation remains unknown. The landscape turns to black when I think of such; a horrid cloud of darkness encompasses my light and lovely colours appear a sort-of depressing grey.
Oh dear, I write like my husband.

Later:

Father found me a lovely pink flower for my hair; I find myself twiddling it nervously as we walk through the town to the Inn. As e're we draw nearer; I find out pace inexplicably quickens - as though the same anxieties push us to haste despite our pronounced lethargy. The long journey has, indeed, made us awash with debilitating tiredness.

"This is the place" Mr Butcher, telegraph in hand, gestures to a white, candlelit building.

"How archaic" says my Father "looks untouched for centuries!"

Admittedly, I was wholly disinterested in the building's exterior - choosing instead to step inside. I believe my Father and Mr Butcher followed me eventually.

The inside was oddly comforting; like a bar from London town only quaint and filled with mysterious locals. I note the staircase to the left of me which must lead to rooms. The downstairs was full of large communal tables; filled with the intoxicated townsfolk which took little interest upon my arrival.

"Yes, Thank you-" I hear a voice behind me - my Father -
"we're looking for a Mr Thomas Thorne."

"Corner" the landlord replies in a curious accent "he expecting
woman."

Instantaneously I look; a rush of fondness encapsulates me as I
gaze upon him. He sits at a table with another man.

"Thomas!" I call (at such volume I startle them both) "my
Love!"

He stands; rushing to me with profound endearment before
promptly kissing me. I blush at such public intimacy; but care
not of making a spectacle. I'd surely die before parting from him
again.

"Catherine- oh, my darling!" Says he, holding my my face "I
cannot believe you-"

"With love's light wings did I o'erperch these walls, for stony
limits cannot hold love out" I say; he smiles fondly at my quote.

"My darling how you must've traveled! And your Father, o'
how I must've worried you and-"

"O, heavens Thomas, none of it matters!" I assure "who is your
friend? Why did you send for us? Lord are you-"

"Nay, nay there's simply too much to disclose tonight."

"Aye, miss" says the other man "we're all tired. Best start
business tomorrow."

"But Thomas-" I gasp "for so long I've awaited your word! You
cannot deny it me after-"

"You've trusted me thus far, my love" my husband concludes
softly "might I ask you continue for one more night?"

I scoff, but with a small smile add "you terrible, terrible men. This better be worth such trouble."

The two men share an unreadable expression.

V

In all honesty Catherine and I haven't a *wink* of sleep last night. I awoke this morning with great reluctantly; my need for enthusiasm fulled solely by my wife's desire for knowledge (and my pressing need to make light of this terrible ordeal - sleep or no; we've wasted far too much time already bringing everyone together.)

I cannot help but feel therefore my sleeplessness was somewhat due to guilt - regret sears my mind with questions; my nightly peace e're set aflame with self-loathing. How could I bring my wife into this terrible mess? The woman whom I vowed to protect henceforth rushing to my aid with nothing but faith? O' heaven let it be known her virtues are too fair for the likes of I; I do believe my wife an angel.

Alas, upon the thought of heaven I'm thus plagued with horrific visions of Isabelle once more - I couldn't save her; what of Catherine if- Oh! What a dammed fool I am! My dreams know such too; thus wrack my consciousness with taunting sleepless. Alone with my thoughts I'm left with no option to suppress them. A weak mind n'er offers strength, after all.

What's done is done; one cannot change the past. At present I will ensure the safety of my wife; my upmost priority! For now, she is by my side. And this ordeal will end with such, verbatim, or may God strike me where I stand.

I cannot dwell on my guilt at present; time simply does not allow for it. I must opine therefore, in aid of morale, that sleeping by her side once more was tremendously up lifting. I cannot voice the extent of my gratitude for her haste - her invariably loyalty is something I've come to appreciate profoundly in recent days.

She's always been so trusting, so caring. My Catherine acts as a beacon of hope in the darkness; a guiding light of virtuous spirits. I've no doubt her goodness shall lift our own tremendously.

****

Upon our entry downstairs, it swiftly dawned on me the tole this situation has taken on everyone. Our party, sat hunched around the breakfast table like lifeless souls as though they hadn't slept in weeks! Humphrey mumbles something inarticulacy that one can only assume was "good morning" as Catherine rubs her eyes with a smile of acknowledgment. Patrick eats with glazed eyes; transfixed e're on his rather lackadaisical breakfast. The only member unaffected appeared to be Catherine's father, but then I suppose a gentlemen of the military would be used to such callous conditions - he sits bold upright, surveying the table with that usual look of inquisition.

"Ah! Morning both" says he haphazardly.

"I trust you didn't sleep either?" His companion opines before gesturing to the Captain "god knows how this one does it, ay?"

"Not a wink" I say, before holding out my hand "My apologies, I'm Catherine's husband. I don't believe we've met?"

He accepts my formality with a chuckle; life seemingly restored as he shakes it rather vigorously "Patrick Butcher; friend of your wife's old man here."

I glance to my wife who covers her mouth in amusement. Her Father straightens his tie indignantly to conceal a small smile which curiously pricks at his lips.

"Right, we all know each other-" Humphrey opines suddenly "now to business-"

"A-uh, on the contrary" the Captain clears his throat, gesturing in the direction of my enigmatic companion "who might you be?"

"Humphrey" says he plainly "Humphrey Bone."

"Friend of yours, Tom?" Asks Patrick.

"Well, after-we-"

I fumble over my words; unsure where to start with this elaborate story. It suddenly dawns upon me how ludicrous the pair of us should sound; how we could possibly expect the others to consider our truth. Catherine must've picked up on my discomfort for she placed a hand on my arm.

"Is something the matter, Thomas?"

I try a smile; but alas this tale allows for none such cheerfulness.

"Forgive me" I say to both her and our party "but I know not where to start- Indeed our tale it-"

The Captain scoffs "From the beginning usually suffices, does it not?"

"I don't think your lady should hear this, Thomas-" Humphrey warns "might she want to-"

"No, I won't be excluded" she asserts rather endearingly, my heart grows fond at the sentiment "if it concerns my Thomas I simply *must* hear it Sir."

"Very well" says he "but I must urge thee to listen with an open mind. I grant you our tale air on the side of unbelievable-"

"Well, try us!" Mr Butcher folds his arms "heavens, we've come this far!"

Humphrey exhales "as you'll have it, sir."

I exhale "Humphrey and myself, of late, have… justifiably, I add… had to flee our original accommodation- the circumstances for such were-"

"Flee?" Humphrey scoffs "Tom, we barley escaped with our *lives*!"

My party let out a simultaneous gasp of horror upon his blunt word; Catherine places a hand to her mouth.

"Oh, my Thomas-!" she glances to me tearfully. I cannot stand her upset.

"Sir!" Her Father urged angrily "I beg you don't be so-"

"You wanted truth. Truth you shall have" opines he indignantly "these past days Thomas has come to bear witness to the terrible order that resides not far from here; a decadent cult of which I've become most intimately acquainted with in my quest to vanquish."

"Vanquish?" Patrick finally questions "cult? Got mixed up with some troublesome locals, did you?"

"Nay sir, far more profound" I justify "these... beings... they lure you in with a false promise of sanctuary. My suspicions were first aroused upon the house's desertion - not a guest in sight! I- I cannot-"

I trail off at the very thought of that shameful encounter; Catherine clutching my arm in fear of my vulnerability. I do wish I could've been braver for her sake.

"There's no euphemism for what we face," Humphrey helps "Thomas and I have first witnessed the start of an epidemic; we've come to appreciate the scope of what threatens humanity-"

Pat shakes his head "what, like influenza?"

"Nay, *nay* sir-" I should've perhaps better sympathised with his ignorance. I was, after all, in the dame situation mere days ago "far worse than any conventional comprehension-"

"These... *beings* you speak of-" the Captain reiterates "it's a war we face? H-how large-"

"We face supernatural warfare sir," says he "the likes of which your society has never seen. We face the takeover of all we hold dear by none other than the occult; an otherworldly terror of fiction - yet a real threat nonetheless!"

"Heavens man," The Captain ushers, we await with baited breath "what in God's name *is* it?!"

Humphrey discloses the likes of vampires and, yet, I find myself emotionless - already numbed to the preposterousness of it all I callously find there scepticism frustrating. For a while; nobody uttered a word. I can only arrive it them trying to comprehend his word. Catherine looks to me wearily; a face of profound horror that unnerves me greatly.

"Is-is it true, Thomas?" She weakly enquires; voice shaken and affrighted "y-your serious, my love?"

"Heavens, Catherine!" Her Father folds his arms "this is clearly some local ploy of folklore! A tourist attraction I- this accusation holds no substance, think rationally!"

"T-there has to be another explanation-" Patrick agrees rather less maliciously "this- this is nowt short of Lunacy, boys! This cult you talk of its- it *can't* be supernatural - an *oddity* aye, but-"

"Cast aside your urban convention" Humphrey gravely concludes "I weren't to believe it. Nor Thomas. But now we see its truth and we urge you to do the same. This threat, unbelievable as it may be, is as real as you or I. And we simply cannot afford to dismiss it for the sake of rationality."

"Have you any proof of these- these-" The Captain trails off; understandably so. I know all too well the extend of duality that must war his thoughts.

"Oh, I've proof."

It is then that Humphrey pulls his shirt to reveal those ghastly puncture wounds that once convinced me of his truth. Both Patrick and the Captain blanche upon morbid realisation.

"Good…God" Catherine's Father breaks a sweat, grasping his chair as our truth dawns upon him in all its troubling strength. To this day I have never seen him so affrighted; his calm visage now awash with fear "are those… is that *real*?"

"Aye. Real as your eyes perceive them, Sir."

Patrick goes to speak; but his weak words are lost to my wife's cry of discomfort. Those telling, bloody pricks in his neck yield the shock value to cause my poor Catherine to faint; our dammed tale having finally taken its tole on her poor, feminine nerve.

"Oh, my Darling!" I cry, holding her tight to my shoulder as the men simultaneously rush to her aid "Alack, Sir! Fetch water!"

I look to my poor girl as Patrick complied; splashing droplets gently on her forehead until she awakes. Wearily; she glances to me - breath slightly laboured from her dreadful shock.

"Are you alright, madam?" Asks Humphrey with marginal guilt; even more so when her Father narrowed his eyes.

"You could've *warned* the poor girl before you-"

"No, Father really I-" I help her sit up "I'm fine. But gentlemen you must understand this, well this is-"

I watch the party gravely nod; understandably re-establishing their own concerns after the momentary distraction. Patrick bows his head as the Captain clears his throat.

"Evidently, this is too much" he asserts "Catherine, you shall hear no more of this. Us gentlemen shall paraphrase in due course."

"But, Father-"

"Listen to me, Kitty" he places a hand to her trembling shoulder "what this man talks of; it's not for the ears of a young woman like yourself."

Wordlessly; she complies with a disgruntled nod. She utters her goodbyes before leaving our table. I saw not exactly what happened; but I turn in response to her apologetic gasp - I can only assume she collided with the gentlemen opposite her in the midst of her restlessness.

"Oh, forgive me" says she haphazardly "I wasn't looking-"

"Quite alright," the gentlemen replies, in that accent I'm swiftly growing accustomed to "express letter for yourself, madam."

She accepts it graciously; counting the journey to her room with new found enthusiasm. I thought it most likely a letter from a companion of some-sorts and thus was glad she might be uplifted by their word.

After my wife was safely out of earshot; I turn my attention back to the table of gentlemen; their countenance in turn each poorly-facading confidence.

I nod to my companion "You may speak plainly now; Humphrey."

Patrick shudders "you *really* speak the truth, Sir?"

"I've no reason to lie" Humphrey replies with earnest solemnity.

"Indeed" The Captain theorised "most definitely not over something, on surface evaluation, ludicrous. I mean- no sane man could fathom such intricate deceit; then again no sane man should believe it!"

"Aye" says he "but only a fool would not act upon this imminent threat."

"So we're either intellectuals or idiots" Patrick shrugs. I must opine I find his humour most comforting amongst the discomfort. After brief laughter from my party; Catherine's father predictably pushes on.

"If these - *vampires* - of whom you speak really do pose such an 'imminent threat'; why in God's name hasn't someone put a stop to it?"

"He's got a point" Mr Butcher agrees "I mean, clues in the name, folklore, been around for donkeys. Why only *now* are we hearing about it?"

Humphrey exhales a grave sigh "For too long as mankind overlooked the unusual; which is why thus far they've been able to walk free and plot their unopposed takeover."

"T-takeover-?" Patrick weakly stutters.

"Aye, Sir" says he "For so long I was alone in my scheme; before I could convey such to yourself. These vampires of whom I speak; they plot to take your London - fill it with their own kind and transgress the population to decadence."

"Good lord" the Captain whispers "but surely we've time before they make such arrangements?"

"On the contrary Sir, they've already a boat," The men's eyes dramatically widen "it waits on the coast until they've right of passage."

Mr Butcher straightens his glasses in desperate attempt to comprehend "a-and how might they get such? Travel card, papers-?"

"Sir lest you forget these are ancient, supernatural beings-" Humphrey scoffs "thousands of years worth of prophecy are hardly likely to be appeased by a mere passport!"

"Then how, dammit?" Catherine's Father pushes irately.

"A binding ritual" I answer "upon the next full moon - am I correct Humphrey?"

"Aye."

"Heavens" Patrick gasps "but that's-"

"Less than two weeks-" The Captain blanches "that's hardly anything- Sir, we've no time to- this is *suicide*! You're asking us to- to go over the top in- that's like if the frontline was one man with a damn stick!"

He rises from his chair in agitation before Patrick pulls him down. The man composes himself; looking to my companion apologetically.

"Forgive me" says he "but you must understand I am hideously out of my depth here. I know nothing of rituals, folklore and- I know not how to prepare for such. We've no *plan*, no-"

"On the contrary Sir," says Humphrey "upon my research I've found this ritual may only he done via blood connections to ancient tombstones. Once done, they are bound to sacred earth and permitted to travel - but trapped here before, like rats."

"I see-" the Captain nods thoughtfully "might there be a way to- to stop this *before* it happens? Whilst we've still the upper hand?

"Destroy the stones, stop the ritual, surely?" I opine.

"Could be right there, Thomas" Patrick points in my direction "where did you say this site was, Humphrey?"

"Regrettably I know not" says he "I was rather hoping-"

"Well" the Captain concludes "you've two weeks to find it. Patrick and I will to the coast; destroy their ship as a last resort."

"N-now sir" Humphrey stumbles "We really ought to-"

"To what? Sit idly by and think of a better idea? I'll be dammed if London society is destroyed due to our lack or pragmatism."

"He's right" I gravely conclude "I grant you this plan... unorthodox; but we're running out of time, Humphrey."

Patrick nods his contribution as my companion paces the room; hand nervously combing his hair in agitated contemplation.

"Fine!" Says he in a reluctant conclusion "if Thomas and I can get the sight's location; this-this might work. I've the directions to the boat; they made me negotiate the damn thing! We'll keep in touch via telegram-"

Humphrey draws a notepad to map the location before handing it solemnly to The Captain.

"Excellent-" says he "tomorrow we'll to-"

His word is interrupted upon Catherine's urgent cry. She rushes to out table seemingly more affrighted than before!

"Mrs Thorne-" says Patrick "are you quite alright-?"

"Oh; heavens-" she pushes the letter into my arms; allowing me to read. I cannot recall reading it in its entirety, only that its contents delay our plans quite significantly.

"We-we must to the asylum" I say "Alison-"

"Alison?" Mr Butcher repeats "who...?"

"Her dear friend - Catherine," her father looks to her sternly "is she alright?"

"I know not" says she "oh, God! I don't think my heart can take any *more* mystery! I must know if- oh, *please*! We *must* go! It's not far from here-"

"We've no *time*" Humphrey urges "we're already-"

"Can't you see the state the poor girls in?!" The Captain barks "your end of our plan holds no substance at present; it would do no harm to accompany her whilst we continue our journey."

Catherine sniffs "Journey? Where are you going, Father?"

With facaded countenance he places a paternal hand on my wife's shoulder; I watch with fondness at his gentle gesture.

"Patrick and I must go to the coast to sort this dreadful mess out" says he "I promise you we'll be quite safe. Thomas and Humphrey will accompany you to the institution tomorrow."

"Thank you" Catherine nods with a sweet smile before returning to her room.

"Now," Patrick shakes his head "that's far from the truth, Sir."

Catherine's Father bows his head with marginal guilt.

"Perhaps" says he "but she'll know in due course. She has far too much to worry about at present."

"We *shall* go tomorrow" Humphrey nods with slightly more sympathy "as you say; we've nothing more to do our end."

"So it's decided-" I shake my party's hands in turn "tomorrow; we split up and begin our plan."

<u>Letter, Dr Micheal Cooper to Mrs Catherine Thorne.</u>

Mrs Thorne,

It is with great reluctance that I request your presence at our institution. On normal circumstances, you understand, our patients are denied non-medical visitation as they haven't the mindset to request such... nor, indeed, to hold civil conversation. The disruption of routine and isolation has proven immensely troubling for my patients - as have the outside world found the institution distressing.

This is not a place for the faint hearted, Mrs Thorne, which Is why I curse upon inviting your goodness to a place like this. On this occasion however; I go against my better judgment. Your dear friend Alison has been invariably insistent in her requests - says it a matter of upmost importance - won't eat or sleep until satisfied.

I do believe she is trying to communicate some form of information; but in her current state madam I simply cannot make heads or tails of it. From a professional perspective I believe your presence would invite new perspective to the matter - perhaps something of her life your intimate acquaintance could contextualise for me? There's something there, I'm sure of it. The consistency of these ravings mark my suspicion that it is more than rambles of lunacy.

I've no doubt your good heart is as curious as I - the case of Miss Alison has proven invariably fascinating in its enigmatic mystery. Above all I do feel sorry her and yourself, Mrs Thorne, for I do understand the upset this situation must be causing you.

Please do not distress yourself too much upon my word therefore, Alison is in no harm bar unsettled aggravation. I sympathise that from London this journey might be too much to ask of you, Madam. I beg you don't feel obligated to comply. If you wish to bring a party for support I can arrange for suitable accommodation my end. It is the least I could offer you for humouring me.

The choice is yours of course, but I do urge you to carefully consider - for both science and empathy's sake this matter is, in my opinion, quite urgent.

With the hopes of meeting in due course,

Dr Micheal Cooper.

VI

I was beyond grateful for the goodness of my Husband and his companion in accompanying me to the Asylum with such haste. With all that has been happening I thought it their last priority to appease my nerve; but their invariable kindness has proven immensely uplifting in my situation - when the time comes, I shall of course seek to do the same.

The journey to Alison's institution was terribly long even with the added proximity of the Button inn - I can scarcely imagine where my thoughts would take me should I have traveled alone from London. Occasionally, in silence, my troubles bring me to ghastly conclusions of which I daren't wish upon a soul...

They say suspension of disbelief warrants blissful ignorance but, as I tell my Husband often, we are not in the Theatre. Although sometimes I deeply wish it weren't real. I find situations most horrid when I have no fact or definitive evidence as it is then one's imagination starts to fill in the blanks. My companions have distracted me somewhat from worry; I have concluded there is nothing to be done until arrival. After all, I could not be more content in the knowledge my dear Alison is in the best hands at present with Dr Cooper.

I mean this not as it sounds; but Humphrey's plan has proven quite brilliantly distracting. Granted, such a terrible, terrible ordeal holds no place in comfort - indeed such a thing as the occult holds no place anywhere, which is why, I'm informed, it must be irradiated - but I find such structure inexplicably stabilising. I was beside myself with hysteria upon the prospect of war and takeover and other ghastly stuff that I beg to be spared of the detail - but knowing a definitive route to its stopping? To know such foulness *can* be stopped? I felt hope, and not just the hope I've been facading out of ignorance, but genuine prosperity. Whether it be male confidence influencing my persuasion I know not, but to know such a grand situation is within the realms of human control? I do believe it puts into perspective my own troubles.

My dear looks to me, in all honesty and openness and says 'Catherine, my love, what we face is beyond comprehension, beyond the likes of believable or fathomable - but we must believe it's truth; believe if there is a battle to be won, we shall win it. If there is an end, we shall be the ones to end it. They hold whatever supernatural power might've befallen them; but we, my dear, hold Righteousness. We've the upper hand, a divine plan of intellectual strategy. With God on our side, we are already victorious.'
O' my darling has always had a way with words. In reference to the divine one cannot help but question how such unpleasant beings were a product of creation; but now of all times (I believe) is *not* a time to question faith. I've faith in their existence just so as the God that adjudicates our success. And that it *will* be, all good things, as I've the Lord and the goodness of my party to depend on. In all faith therefore, my optimism puts my worries to rest as we approach our destination; indeed, I should be some terrible hindrance if all I can contribute is unjustified pessimism.

Later: It is awfully late when we arrive; my Husband and Mr Bone appear equally weary as we had spent the entirely of the day travelling. I am thankful we could arrive by nightfall, but I must add that the present darkness does not lend itself to enhancing appearance. The Asylum looked terribly frightening upon our arrival; the building's harsh, antiquated features appeared errily haunting when lost to the blackness. I am only thankful the lack of light concealed any additional horrors we should encounter.

Dr Cooper waits on the driveway as our coach enters the gate; he takes my hand, most gentlemanly, as I exit.

"Mrs Thorne" says he with remarkable cheerfulness, it is evident that his vocation's dreariness has little effect on his demeanour "I cannot thank you enough for coming."

"Indeed, it is my husband and his companion that you should thank" I reply "they, after all, were kind enough to accompany me."

"Ah, Mr Thorne" says he, shaking Thomas' hand before turning to Mr Bone "Dr Cooper. And yourself?"

"Humphrey bone" says he "the moral support, if you will."

"Kind indeed Sir. Now! It'll do little good to Alison should we all catch our deaths-" he walks us to the doorway "this way, if you please."

The inside of his establishment is similarly dimly-lit; it holds little splendour but tasteful class. The lobby is relatively bare; but then again I suppose visitation is few and far between as per the qualms of his letter. There is a small, narrow staircase that I assume leads to his living accommodations. To my right, a corridor with signposts to his patient's respective patient's wards. We pause at the reception desk.

"Indeed" the man smiles, a wicked little smile "I suppose we ought to wait for Doctor cooper now."

I laugh; but it takes my party a moment to register his jest. His wit is a trait I quickly grew accustomed to through his letters; I oft' feel the extent of such is repressed. Whilst I admire him for his humorous approach to such a taxing job (and indeed, making light of out own situation) I equally appreciate his need to maintain professionalism.

"I jest, gentlemen" he laughs "apologies if in poor taste. I've become a bit... desensitised, so to speak."

My Thomas chuckles in response "Indeed, Sir you're forgiven! I do believe a laugh is exactly what the Doctor ordered for my dear Catherine. She's been awfully uneasy upon your word."

"Yes, How is Alison?" I enquire "pray, when can I see her? Is she well?"

The Doctor snickers at my rambles, indeed I must appear so terribly impatient "as well as a madwoman can be, m'lady. I shan't trouble you with detail at this hour; I do believe yourself and your companions must be awfully tired from the journey?"

"We haven't traveled far" I plead "only a day, we've not from London."

"Oh?" He grimaces "I do apologise if I've ruined a holiday-"

"Sir, this *is* a holiday in comparison" Mr Bone opines with a crude little snicker "but I thank you for your understanding; I believe rest is in order."

"Indeed-" my Husband turns to me "I've no doubt we'll see Alison tomorrow. She's probably sleeping now, my love. We ought not to wake the poor girl."

"All patients are asleep, madam" the Doctor smiles reassuringly "best you do the same. Up the stairs, there are two spare rooms to your left."

"Most kind Sir," I say, the gentlemen nod in similar thanks.

"Least I could do" says he earnestly.

Humphrey Bone's Journal, 1st October.

Last night's sleep was by no means revolutionary; justifiably, admittedly. I haven't a good night's rest in considerable time. I cannot help but fear we are wasting valuable time with this queer side quest but, as Catherine's father rightly opined, we've nothing better to do at present. Her happiness therefore validates this trip.

The Doctor is pleasant company; his humour is in good taste - now more than ever can I appreciate it. I'm yet to meet the other staff bar a couple of attendants I've acknowledged in passing - the poor man must be terribly busy with all these patients.

I do admire him; this asylum is awfully bleak although I've n'er seen the man's smile faulter. Indeed, one is inclined to think it a facade for Mrs Thorne's sake - the poor girl must be worried sick about her dear friend - but, again, one appreciates the sentiment. In times of dark you ought to cease any speck of light you can get your hands on - even from unlikely sources. I don't believe I'm the only one to find this visit pleasantly, if not momentarily, distracting.

The Doctor, true to his word, took us to see this Alison immediately after breakfast - pleasant, for such an institute - he lead us to the appropriate corridor with haste I did not anticipate. His countenance evident that perhaps this matter is more serious than first anticipated.

The corridors themselves were plain; leading to roomy cells and additional staff that monitor the patient's activity. One cannot help but note the layout resembles more of a prison...

The inhabitants become restless upon our arrival; Dr cooper instructs us to ignore these senseless rambles and agitation as we continue past. Some hang on the bars, making primitive noises at such volume that I couldn't help but turn my head. If, indeed, 'senseless rambles' are the criteria for madness; I wonder how long we should explain our situation to Dr Cooper before we are similarly locked up! I do feel for these patients, indeed society has successfully vilified what all the population suffers from - some are just better at hiding it than others.

"She's is in here, madam" the Doctor gestures to the left, a woman in dirty overalls sits quietly on her cell's bench "Alison, you have some visitors."

The women glances up, smiling most hysterically before standing to clasp the bars. It would be false to say her demeanour did not disturb me - there was an element to her visage that made us all profoundly uneasy.

"Kitty!" She grins rather manically "Kitty! It's you, Kitty Kitty cat!"

Alison paces the cell; muttering Mrs Thorne's name gleefully as though as a chant. Dr Cooper exhales, rubbing his temples with exasperation as my party watch this spectacle.

"Alison-" he finally calls "calm down. We talked about this."

"Oh, yes!" Says she "oh yes oh yes we did! It's very exciting Doctor, very exciting!"

"Mrs Thorne wants to talk to you, Alison."

Tentatively, Catherine approaches her cell with her Husband close behind her. She smiles at Alison, clearly a front for her uneasiness.

"Hello, Alison" says she "how are you?"

"Oh, very well, thank you."

The coherence of her response evidently took the Doctor off guard quite significantly.

"Yes-" adds Thomas "we've been awfully-"

"Shush, you" the girl snaps "I'm talking. Bloody rude!"

He backs away at this response, sensibly choosing to stand by my side as the two women continue their conversation.

"Now, Alison my dear" Catherine shakes her head "you ought not to speak to my husband in such a way."

"Oh, I'm sorry Kitty" says she with yet another abrupt shift in her demeanour "It's been a while since I've spoken to others."

"Oh, Alison" Catherine replies, disheartened "how awful it must be - all this time!"

"Oh, it's not so bad when she talks to me!"

Catherine tilts her head "*she*? Pray, who-"

"This 'Grey Lady' figure" Dr Copper informs us "she supposedly speaks to Alison quite often - different messages, the same hallucination. Eerily consistent, if you ask me."

"She's got a message for *you* this time, Kitty" says the patient gleefully "that's why I simply had to see you. It's urgent, you know."

"A message?" The Doctor enquires "you never told me, Alison?"

She folds her arms indignantly "That's because it's not *for* you. Top secret. For the cat's ears only."

Dr Cooper nods as Alison beckons mrs Thorne closer.

Catherine inhales with understandable trepidation "And... what does she say?"

The girl flashes that maniac grin once more; tugging at her hair whilst pacing the length of her cell.

"Ancient site, ancient man. Old fool. That's where you'll find those bloody stones!" she pauses, as if to listen "he owns their ritual grounds! Yes, he does! He does! She says so - you're running out of time though, folks! Blood will spill, then they bind, then set sail, London find-"

Blood will spill, then they bind, then set sail, London find.

She repeats this morbid line whilst pacing the floor; quickening the pace in a spiral of madness that I care not of; her words send a profound chill through my person for they grant a remarkable similarity to our own predicament. How, indeed, I know not. But then again to question what is fathomable at this stage would be terribly foolish. I feel my eyes widen; by some force of curiosity I approach the bars of her cell. She watches me do so, neither of us speak so much as observe one another with unspoken perplexity. Her words astound me, truly, and I do believe Thomas felt the same. I look over my shoulder at his affrighted expression before Catherine grasps my sleeve to signify her own discomfort. Dr Cooper remains in the dark; but his visage tells me this is the first he's heard of such too.

"And who is this man?" I finally blurt from overwhelming urgency "you say - the Grey Lady says - he owns this sight?"

Despite playing to her lunacy; the woman does not respond. Instead, she folds her arms as if theatrically displeased. Alison shakes her head, humming a tune I do not recognise.

"She won't tell you" she sings, her tone vexingly teasing like a petulant child "not *you-*"

"But she'll tell me, won't she Alison?" Catherine smiles - clever girl - "I'd like to know where this site is too."

"Barkley" says she, wide-eyed as if possessed before a wide grin spreads across her face "Barkley-something. West coast; where the sun sets and the full moon rises - not long now! Not long at all! Then they'll set sail - the owl, and my Kitty Cat, went to sea- "

Alison mumbles some rendition of 'the owl and the pussycat', her coherency evidently ceased. Catherine turns to me, distressed, but not nearly to the same extent of Dr Cooper - the poor man had blanched quite considerably.

"Barkley-?" I repeat "that gives us-"

"Beg-Chetwynde" the Doctor all but whispers "Barclay Beg-Chetwynde. his family have owned land on the Binat border for generations."

Thomas falters "Binat? but that's-"

"The West of Transylvania" I nod "aye."

"I-I'm sorry gentlemen-" the Doctor shudders "I must ask you to go. This- this investigation is of great importance-"

The man turns to leave; but something desperate in me grabs his sleeve.

"Sir-" I plead "this really is *very* important."

"Yes Doctor" Thomas opines; manoeuvring himself in front of the poor man to block his exit "we simply *must* know more!"

"I-I'm sorry" says he "but these rambles have too much correlation for coincidence- I cannot afford to waste any time investigating why. Please, excuse me."

Doctor Cooper begins to walk the corridor; I immediately follow with Thomas and his wife close behind me.

"Doctor-!" I clutch his shoulder in desperation "at least tell us how you know this man!"

"I said good day-!"

"*Please*" Catherine finally insists, with enough sweetness to melt the coldest of hearts "please, spare a moment for Alison."

Slowly, Dr Cooper exhales "His wife was a patient here. Barkley's wife, that is."

I nod "so that's the relation to Alison? How she knows this man?"

"Couldn't be" he shrugs with exasperation "she came in for Alcoholism two years before - their paths never crossed! I-I don't understand it-"

"This- site of which she speaks" says Thomas, ignoring the poor man's uneasiness "what's it like?"

"Old" he blankly replies "what more is there to say? It's- originally an ancient burial ground. Tomb stones, expansive acres - that sort of thing. The whole things been preserved quite immaculately."

I catch my companion's eye at that moment; it is evident our thoughts align. This description matches my research practically verbatim. Granted, such may be coincidence, but we simply could not afford to dismiss it. By now we're so submerged in the supernatural 'returning now would be as tedious as to go over.' Thus, one thinks it valid to persist.

"And where might we find it, Sir?" I ask with appeasing caution

"Christ sakes!" The Doctor shakes his head angrily, evidently tiring of our relentless inquisition "I'm not at liberty to say Sir that's- it's confidential information. Now, please, you've kept me from my studies long enough!"

The man turns on his heels, continuing down the corridor. In that moment I do believe it stalemate.

"Shame" says Catherine suddenly, with enough volume so the man might hear "I would've loved to send a letter."

The Doctor turns his head skeptically "*letter?*"

"Oh yes" says she with quite remarkable quickness "I wish to write to this 'Barkley' - perhaps see if he knows anything about Alison. Something that could... help."

He raises an eyebrow "and this is all?"

She smiles "Of corse Sir. Nothing more."

"I shall look through the records for the address madam" he turns to leave once more "tell me if you find anything, would you?"

"Oh, of course, Doctor."

As he walks away, back turned, I notice the girl's fingers crossed behind her back. This wicked wit of Catherine's is a side to her I should like to see more of. Her husband glances to me, smiling, as if to say she's done it. We've got a lead.

Telegram - Thomas Thorne to Patrick Butcher.

We've had a revelation our end - I do believe we've secured the location for this ritual sight - a gentleman owns land on the Binat border that fits the description perfectly. How we acquired such would surly lend to scepticism, so I shall spare you the detail in aid of maintaining focus. Catherine, Humphrey and myself plan to travel and complete the plan.

The address is disclosed below; I shall update you in due course if we succeed in destroying the ritual stones. In case of out error or failure, I must urge you to continue with plan B as previously arranged.

Telegram - Patrick Butcher to Thomas Thorne

Excellent news! I shall update the Captain; he shall be pleased we can progress (he asks after Catherine, incidentally). We're due to arrive at the coast in two days - Humphrey's directions were relatively easy to follow.

The Captain said it would be worth checking the cargo as well - find something of interest? More clues perhaps?

We'll meet you in Binat once we've finished our end. Good luck you you, God bless.

VII

The sun had long since set by the time we arrived at the coast; the driver would take us no further than the town centre and so Patrick and I made our own way to the beach.

Thankfully, the worst of the weather had subsided by the evening - but I must admit the winds were still oddly strong. Our carriage nearly blew over in the worst of it earlier, and even then as I walked we oft' had sand blown in our faces by harsh, unforgiving gusts - as though nature itself was taunting us. ~~I have to say, if one were to believe in omens, this blatant opposition was surely not good sign~~. Luckily however, we hadn't walked far before the docks came to view. We then, of course, knew we were close.

Naturally, the area was deserted at this hour; I could hear nothing but the eerie creaks of fishing boats tied haphazardly to rotting platforms. The atmosphere here much reminded me of my night watch in the Crimea - desolate and oddly tranquil yet with an element of impending danger that kept my reflexes sharp. The night was similarly cold too, I notice Patrick shiver as he wraps his coat tighter.

"I say, Captain" Pat calls, his breath visible as he exhales "What exactly is it we're looking for?"

"A small vessel, supposedly" I reply "only non-commercial boat in the lot. Shouldn't take too long to find."

"Right. She got a name?"

"Yes-" I tilt the paper, squinting at Mr Bone's Hand "*Carmilla*."

As I predicted, we find their transportation in no time at all - the boat sits just beyond the main docks, anchored in isolation at the end of the walkway. Her hull was blood read and rusty in colour, relatively small but enough to cast an uninviting shadow on the damp wood we stand on. The two of us take in the sight, suddenly unnerved by the task at hand.

"Well, here we are" I point to her name on the side of the hull.

"They've actually helped us out here," Patrick chuckles, gesturing to the empty waters "parked her far enough away so that we won't damage anything else."

"Yes" I nod "I suppose so."

He then turns to me, rummaging around in his pocket before drawing a box of matches "suppose we ought to just... get on with it then?"

"Well, hold on old chap" I assert "shouldn't we check the cargo first? There might be something of interest aboard!"

"Sorry! Yes- you're right" he places them back in his coat with haste "it's been a long night I-er- got a little excited."

"understandable" I smile "I too would like to leave as soon as possible. Now, shall we?"

I gesture to the ship's ladder, to which we both clamber aboard - quite the task for both of us, I might add - regrettably I am not as fit as I used to be. Regardless, once on the deck we find a hatch which we mutually assumed led to the cargo below.

Patrick's Journal, 2nd/3rd October

In all honesty I hadn't a clue what we'd find in the hold - and I'd scarcely like to pen all of my suspicions. I could sense the Captain's own trepidation as we descended; we were both awash with a terrible sense of dread that my feeble lantern did little to alleviate.

We've little knowledge of the occult after all; I feared for an awful moment that they should have some advanced weaponry or traps for trespassers such as ourselves. Luckily, there was nothing of the sort - but this uncertainty is sure to return at every obstacle. Even with the Captain's expertise we still could be a poor fit to fight these supernatural beings as, simply, none of us have ever faced such a battle before - let alone have suitable combat training! They say there's nowt more valuable than experience so, by that logic, our group's as cheap as dirt when the going gets tough…

Dwelling on our inadequacy doesn't help things at present however. I creep forward to join the Captain who surveys what looks like infinite boxes - all of which made of similar material yet sized miscellaneously as though to cram everything in any container available.

I chuckle, gesturing to our discovery "you'd have thought someone would've told them they ought to pack light, ay?"

"Indeed" says he with a small smile.

"Well, no point us just standing here" I approach the boxes as confidently as this situation allowed "lets take a look-"

With some effort, The Captain and myself manage to prise open a box. To my dismay (or, more realistically, my relief) they were filled with nothing but earth. Plain earth, as if shoved neat and crammed into these boxes. We exchange a glance which conveys our mutual confusion before opening another to, naturally, be met with the same fate. I won't try to decipher why this was the case, nor why our enemy would need such a thing as

I think I'd go mad should I try. These beings do not follow our ways of conventional, far from it, their queer cargo seems oddly fitting.

"What do you think it's for?" The Captain finally enquires "I- I don't know what to make of this-"

I shrug "Buggered if I know. Then again, it's not really worth questioning things now, is it?"

"No-" he takes a final, curious inspection before closing the box "I suppose not -but, but this is all a bit-"

I believe I cocked my head "a bit *what*?"

"Strange-? Unorthodox-?" The Captain shakes his head, distress creeping into his countenance "I- boxes of earth it- it makes no sense! This is ludicrous!"

I watch as the man turns to leave, hastily returning to the deck as I follow.

"Captain-" I call "are- are you alright?"

"Yes, Patrick I just-" he pauses on the ladder, looking to me with a surprisingly frightened expression "we've no idea what we're dealing with!"

"Well, no-" I shrug "I suppose we don't but-"

"But that's the point!" We're on the docks again; The Captain paces uneasily with his pipe in hand "everything's so enigmatic so- nonsensical, these beings have no pattern, no discernible motif I just - I can't decipher *anything*!"

"Well, Mr Bone knew about their plan for travel" I appease "that's why we're here."

"Yes but what then, Patrick? We blindly follow into battle? What if those boxes mean something - what if they plan something we can't predict?"

"Well, we don't *know* that-"

"But that's just my point again!" He continues to pace "we don't know anything, not even how to *kill* the damn things!"

"Well, Humphrey said wooden stakes should suffice-"

"And who is this *Humphrey*, anyway?" He says, exasperated "I-we hardly know the man yet trust his every word! To travel across some eastern land, to *burn* a ship no less?! To- to face this supposed occult with nothing but damn tent pegs?! How- you must understand, Patrick, I'm used to war, strategy, not a rag-tag bunch of-"

I clutch his shoulder "I know, Theodore, I know. But right now we've a mission - an odd mission granted - but if we can help them surly that's enough?"

"But what *then*?" He sighs "we finish up here and go to -they've never faced combat! Dammit *I've* never faced-"

"And you're right in what you say, this ain't your average fight. All the more reason why we need your expertise! We can *win* this-"

"Patrick" his voice all but trembles, vulnerability fronting to an extent I've never seen before "I'm-I'm *not* in control here. I can't- what if something happens what if- I can't risk Catherine getting hurt, not for -we've no idea what we're up against what if... what if I can't *protect* everyone? What then?"

"Captain-"

"I'm supposed to be the *leader*-" he fumbles, distressed "dammit I'm not even on the front line I'm-I'm out here on plan B miles away from-"

"Ted, Ted!" I shake his shoulders until his muttering ceases, but even then I don't let go "we're in this *together*, alright?"

"But-what if-"

"To hell with the 'what if's'!" I shout - at such volume it catches us both off guard "there's always going to be a 'what if' even if your the most prepared person on earth! Now, I might be too optimistic for you, but I've faith. Might not mean much to you, but it does to me, alright?"

"But how can you be certain?" He shakes his head "hope has no *substance* it's -it's a stab in the dark-"

"*Stake* in the dark" I correct with a snicker "and I'm not. But no one ever is which… which is why there's hope. And if I'm wrong, at least we *tried* - and that's a lot bloody better than anyone else can say!"

"But- trying isn't *winning*-"

"No," I assert, clutching his arm "trying is *believing*."

I then meet his gaze, and in that moment I believe we were thinking alike - so I let him turn his head, abashed, as he always does. Wordlessly, I smile, wishing one day my soldier might win his final battle.

"…You're right, Patrick" says he finally "I believe we *can* do this. We might not know what we're up against - but neither do they! Right now we're all we've got and-and I've faith that that's enough."

"That's good enough for me."

As if to prove my point I light a match at last, throwing it with all my might at the boat's deck. She's set aflame almost instantaneously, the two of us watch in wonder as the fire grows, e're expanding like our rage against the occult. Flames prick impishly at the inky black as scorched wood begins to tumble from the wreckage.

"Thus the battle commences" the Captain says, the light flickering on his stern visage "best head to the frontline."

We walk away, side by side. Burning embers prick the corner of my glasses, a reminder that even if I can't see it; there is a light in the darkness - much like the Captain is to me. Slowly therefore, we walk the beach, the bat that flitters above my head calls the night to full effect.

Julian Fawcett's journal, 2nd/3rd October.

He lay me down that night as always, the carnal urges that course through our veins fronting once more in the form of something beautiful. Robin n'er fails to satisfy, really, we play our little games in satin sheets as though sex was going out of fashion.

The two of us are much alike with our insatiable appetite - Mary too - I oft' see her titillation at the prospect of profane indulgence. Her womanhood holds not the virtue of suppression, instead, the voluptuous sexuality of some wicked temptress. She'll sometimes lie by my side, pleasuring herself to the sounds of our own primitive decadence. Breasts that the two of us have oft kissed do but rapidly heave as laboured breath signifies her climax, ravenous thrusts e're edging me toward my own.

Tonight however, it is just Robin and I - he straddled atop' - muscular thighs crushing my waist. His sharp teeth were hitched to my neck with such passion, such bestial enthusiasm it felt like the first time he'd done so - then again, it always does. His impish tongue moves to my chest, manhood buried deep inside me in aid of seeking my blissful satisfaction. His tongue laps insistently at the redness that oozes from my punctured flesh; his sadistic arousal evident by that gravelly laugh that never fails to make me twitch. I groan, he does the same, holding me then so tenderly I hadn't the discipline to suppress a whimper. The man's thumbs brush my nipples as I arch my back with intemperate want. I am his, *always*, and I crave nothing more than to be used, filled to the brim with his bestial ways. Robin fuels my senses until he is all that I feel, see, *taste*.

It's times like these, pinned underneath my lover in eternal tryst, that I wonder how life would be should I have n'er transgressed - should our hearts never beat as one, our blood n'er mixed. The thought of such a profound loss is enough to end me - for I need it, *him* - my body made for his enjoyment, the boundaries of mortal flesh thus destroyed in divine connection. I cannot deny that I'm addicted to our act; I long for such with unquenchable appetite. That is why we must fulfil this ritual, so that the population once blinded by convention can *feel* as we feel.

"Oh-Robin-" I say, seeing stars once more, they prick at the corner of my eyes like my tears of blissful indulgence "*please*-"

And then we're floating again, I can touch the icy crystals of our bedroom chandelier, and I shan't fall so long as he holds me. I see nought but constellations, the screws of arousal e're tightening, ascending, as I lock eyes with the man that would surely take me to heaven. Robin flashes me a sultry grin before quickening his pace against that spot that drives me positively mad.

"You nearly there now, aren't you-?" he growls through gritted teeth - my current state did not allow for an intelligible reply.

"Yes-" he holds my thigh aloft, grasping it with a clawed hand whilst the other continues to graciously palm my shaft "yes, Robbie, *yes*-!"

"Go on then-" he simply smirks "make it pretty for me."

Robin catches my cries in a kiss, the gesture enough for my love to spill violently over his attentive hand as my ardent finale. My lover follows suit with a muffled curse - our bodies shaking, panting as we gently fall to the bed - carnal urges subdued, for tonight, as the beast falls limp on my chest.

Or, rather, this is what I expect. But instead Robin lifts his head - eyes narrowed as his gaze sears tellingly into my own.

"What is it-?" I can all but slur "what's the matter?"

My lover sits up with troubling haste "something… *wrong*. Can sense it."

"…What is?" I ask with trepidation "Robin-?"

I do not doubt this feeling he oft' gets - his senses are like that of a wolf hunting prey. Collecting myself, I sit up to face him.

"Can't tell - is too far away" he leaves our bed before slowly walking towards the window, his bare figure quite exquisite in starlight "need go… *investigate*."

"What, now?" I know he hears the disappointment that creeps into my voice "can't you come back to bed?"

"No-Julian, this… this *bad*."

"… how '*bad*'?"

"Don't know" he grunts - uneasy, I can tell "that's why I need go."

I hold myself uncomfortably as he watches me "but… you'll be back, won't you Robbie?"

"Yes, Julian-" he presses a reassuring kiss to my lips before walking to the window once more "*promise*. you stay here, alright?"

He then pulls the balcony windows open before transforming, the night air harsh and unforgiving against my bare skin. I pull the thin sheets that flail against the wind over myself for modesty, watching the distinctive silhouette of a bat against the near full moon before my lover is lost to the darkness.

Later: It must've been three or four hours before Robin returned - the early hours of the morning were yet to creep past the horizon as the sky remained encompassed in darkness. I wasn't *worried*, I knew he'd be fine - but I'll admit such a sudden departure did warrant some uneasiness.

Suddenly, Robin's silhouette appears at the window once more - his eyes like beastly sapphires piercing through the inky blackness. Wordlessly, he walks towards me; he is naked yet with not a trace of vulnerability. I shudder at the sight, submissively aroused by the paragon of masculinity; Robin's omnipresent shadow encompassing the room as his person is once again illuminated by the moonlight behind him.

"You're back" I say, standing as he pauses at the foot of our bed "is everything alright now? You were gone for a-"

His expression remains grave and so I trail off, trying to gauge his visage (which appears awash with upset.)

"Robin-? I walk over to him, holding his shoulder "what is it?"

"They've… burnt it. Burnt it *all*."

He looks to me then with a snarl, anger fronting as he tears away from me.

"Burned what? What's the *matter*?!"

"The ship-" he growls "two men, saw em' walking away from the wreckage."

"But how did they-" I pause, locking eyes with my lover who I know shares my worry "you don't think their working with-?"

"They've got to be, Julian!" Says he, agitated "who else would? This- if they've worked out then- I *have* to protect stones-"

Robin makes for the window before I catch is arm "not *now*, Robin, the sun!"

"Always with the fucking sun!" He attempts to tear his arm away but I hold it tight in desperate attempt to make him stay "I'll find shelter - I must go Julian! Let me go!"

"Not on your own-" I plead "they'll *kill* you! Let me come too, I'll-"

"No!" He snarls, still trying to outwit my grasp "already told you can't- can't *lose* you."

He then stops fighting; instead he looks into my affrighted gaze before his eyes soften. Wordlessly, he leans into me, kissing my lips as though it were the last time. I close my eyes tightly, Robin holds the back of my head as if he feared I should disappear. My moans of desperation were all but lost in his mouth as he deepens the kiss, savouring every second. After some time, we pull away.

"You could lose me in five minutes or five centuries" I say, foreheads together in a tender show of affection "but you'll certainly lose me if you go alone. Whatever they're planning - we can *win* this."

"Julian-" says he uncharacteristically softly "Julie, *please*, you don't know what doing-"

"Maybe I don't" I smile "but they for certain don't know what the hell they're up against. I'm not giving up on our dream, alright?"

He nods, a small smile tugging at the corner of his mouth "alright. We go tomorrow."

"…And then?"

"We been checked. It our move now, and we going for mate."

Telegram, Patrick Butcher to Mr Thomas Thorne.

Completed things our end, now headed to Binat to meet you there. Hope all is well - will be seeing you shortly.

VIII

To Sir,

I hope this letter finds you well. Indeed, you do not yet know me, but my name is Thomas Thorne.
I beg you, do not become alarmed upon my word as I offer to you what our industry would consider a rather extraordinary opportunity:

Myself and my acquaintance's are field historians for the new Eastern exhibit in *The Natural History Museum*, London, and your land has been recommended to us as a sight of significant historical value. Our experts have drawn the conclusion that your estate is home to an ancient ritual sight, of which our team should cherish the chance to investigate.

Of course Sir, should you let us do so, your estate and name would be heavily credited in our research and the name 'Beg-Chetwynde' would henceforth be commonly uttered between staff and visitors alike. In addition, we intend to show our gratitude financially with the offer of profit from our exhibition - site such as these, I'm sure you'll know, hold great value.

Our excavation would not take long - we merely wish to gather information on the estate and take some architectural samples. I shall send only myself and two others so our research shan't be invasive or overbearing; your time is important to us.

Your express permission would not go unappreciated Sir, we urge you to carefully consider this opportunity as it should reward you handsomely.

Yours sincerely,

Thomas Thorne, *The Natural History Museum.*

To Mr Thorne,

Under normal circumstances I wouldn't have just anyone pocking around my land - I have had several museums offer similar you understand, bunch of amateur types that know nothing of history and so I turned them all away with their clumsy chisels.

However, your offer intrigued me Mr Thorne. It's not about the money, naturally, but I will put you in touch with my bank in due course. Have you any idea of sums? I should like to know (for my own amusement.)

It just so happens that I've had ideas for the name of the exhibit - one thinks it should have my name, don't you think? You'll agree I'm sure. I shan't be in this week as Bunny (that is, my wife) and myself (Barkley Beg-Chetwynde) have gone to Tuscany. It's only a small estate, a hundred acres or so but it should suffice as a quaint holiday retreat. I trust your team to make a good job of the Beg-Chetweynde estate whilst we're away - I urge you to leave no stone unturned (so to speak) - wouldn't want to miss anything valuable - to the museum, of course.

I look forward to discussing your findings upon my return.

Yours,

Barkley Beg-Chetwynde.

<u>Thomas Thorne's Diary, 4th October</u>.

In all honesty Catherine's idea to charade as archeologists was nothing short of a stroke of genius. I didn't think my Wife's temperament capable of such deceitfulness, but this ordeal has shown sides of her that I've never seen (and, admittedly, am rather enjoying.) I too have found myself acting with more uncustomary behaviour, but then again one supposes these trying times are quite the test of true intent.

I must opine my conscience is not free from guilt, indeed, the idea of promising this man fame and fortune only to have him find his estate destroyed upon his return did warrant some… dithering. I cannot help but feel as though our malicious intent reflects the very beings we wish to destroy! As we approach Binat I do think our actions have rendered our cause some terrible hypocrisy. Doubt creeps e'er closer like some great storm cloud and I wonder, amidst it all, what Isabelle should think of me now.

There is, however, one thing that separates us from our enemy - and that is righteousness. Our actions are justified by the divine wish, God's wish, and we his ministers. Regardless of what it takes we must eradicate the threat for the greater good. And, besides, it is not as though we take from he who cannot afford the loss. We never deceived after all - this is an investigation of sorts - we merely refrained from disclosing the entirety of our purpose.

Note: perhaps minor deceit in vocation…

Both myself and my party are anxious for this dreadful escapade to be over - but then again what we have thus far witnessed will make it horribly difficult to re-integrate within society. For the rest of civilisation shall never know what we did for them - nor believe us should we tell them. Doubt lingers in the back of my mind that should we succeed, should we vanquish these beings - will it be the end? I hardly think the entirety of their species resides in that damnable guesthouse. What if we cannot stop the next time?

Damn this speculation. For now, we've a task. And Humphrey urges me to think of it as one for the greater good of humanity. Perhaps this man has warped my christian morals for the worst but then much like the lord we work in mysterious ways. If one can banish the occult with a sacrifice of mere architecture I know you'd be a damn fool to think twice about it. After all; what's a couple stones to save life as we know it?

Julian Fawcett's Journal, 4th October.

The journey to Binat was… bloody unpleasant to say the least. With Humphrey gone we had to search town for a suitable driver - luckily we found a man who didn't with to be payed upfront (damn fool, perfect for our plan, really).

We've had to wear what the modern men wear too, Mary insisted we must at least try to blend in (well, as well as we could with dark umbrellas in broad daylight.) I believe we looked a right spectacle in those tight, modest garments - but I suppose at least we passed as rich eccentrics.

The fabric wasn't nearly revealing enough in my opinion - nor breathable - I oft' found myself laughing at Robin's futile attempt to loosen that horrid frilly collar, hair haphazardly tied back in a ponytail. I thought it nice to see more of his face, but my lover didn't seem to share my enthusiasm. Mary wore one of those 'corsets' that pushed her breasts to the front, not all bad, I suppose. Myself? I wore stockings under my trousers just for the hell of it… might make a long journey more interesting, anyway.

Enough of curious fashions, we've more to think about at present. Even as our carriage draws e'er nearer to Binat I wonder what we should find? Exactly how much damage has the poet done? Thus far we've been content in the knowledge that no one would believe him, but what if we're wrong? Never for a second did I think he'd follow through with any antagonisation - let alone recruit accomplices! The scenery flashes past the windows and I feel less and less in control, as though we're rats being lured into some sort of trap.

"What's the matter?" Robin places a hand on my thigh, the driver does not notice "been staring for a while now."

"It's nothing, really," I try "I've just… I've got a bad feeling about all this."

"Well" he squeezes my hand, smiling "me haven't got particularly *good* feeling about this either. Never great sign when someone set your stuff on fire."

"What do you thinks will happen?" Mary asks from opposite "won't be too…"

"Nah, won't be too bloody" my lover reassures "us three should be enuff' to scare them off. Probably only take a couple' transformations then they'll be runnin' like before - only this time, they won't be back. Nobody need get hurt."

"Shame" I pout "I was rather looking forward to sinking my teeth into something."

Robin growls, whispering "can bite me anytime-"

I turn to him, creeping onto his lap all the while we whisper unseemly nothings into each-other's necks. My lover goes to unbutton my shirt before Mary coughs, gesturing to our thankfully ignorant driver. Wordlessly therefore we extract ourselves - I must remember such display, especially in our circumstances, might not always be welcomed by their type.

Robin adjusts his collar "right- where were we?"

"Bloodshed" I recall "…or lack of."

Mary shrugs "Doesn't have to be. Can do the ritual when we be ridded' of them. Then things get bloody."

"Might as well, suppose we there already" Robin nods with a snicker "guess those idiots actually helped us out."

"Helped out with what, ay?" Our driver enquires - nosey bastard "you lot off to a costume party?"

"That's it sweetheart" I dismiss before turning my attention back to our conversation. Robin continues:

"Might not even *be* there. I mean, they burn boat, might've only done that cuz' they don't know about stones. And even if they did *and* knew where find them, there very little chance they destroy em' as well."

"That's a point-" I shrug "well, either way we'll be there to protect them should they-"

"Ah!" Our driver looks over his shoulder, still evidently mulling over our previous exchange "so that's why you're dressed as a camp sort-of caveman Sir!"

Robin snarls, bearing those pearly daggers as I instinctively place my arm over his chest. I kiss his nape when the man's back is turned again, and Robin slumps back against the chair, evidently defeated. I find it quite amusing that this should be the only way to tame the beast.

For the moment, I am confident what we face is within our control. My trepidation has been suppressed by the knowledge that we've the upper hand - or more importantly, the powers to acquire such should the situation arise.

"Eh, how long left?" Robin calls "recon we be there soon?"

"Cripes, you even sound like one!" I do wish the man would shut up - otherwise he most certainly won't make it to Binat "not long now, Sir - can tell by the mountains."

"It be true-" Mary points to the window "we be not at home anymore."

Later: the evening draws near as we arrive in the main town Binat, yet another advantage for us - the setting sun only renders us stronger. The three of us turn to the window as the carriage comes to a halt, our driver opens the left door before clearing his throat.

"Right, here we are-" says he, I knew then exactly that he wanted "so, if you wouldn't mind-"

I look to my lover who simply smirks - that wicked glint in his eyes wordlessly conveys I'll like the outcome should I follow his lead.

The man continues "is *someone* going to pay me?"

"No can do" Robin grins with taunting smugness.

"Yes; impossible I'm afraid" I shrug indifferently "haven't got any."

It is then the driver's expression shifts. In a fit of anger he grasps Robin's collar, pulling him to his scrunched face.

"No money?!" The man growls "look, I don't know what you think you're playing at, but if I don't get payed someone's going to get hurt-"

It is evident his intimidation tactics are ineffective - Robin's smile remains plastered on his face.

"Well," he says, tapping the driver patronisingly on the nose "it not like you be needing any."

"What the bloody hell are you talking about?!" He pulls him tighter, so much so that I have to refrain from interfering. As much as it pains me to watch Robin's face tells me he's in control. He's most likely enjoying being handled so roughly "is this a fucking *joke* to you? Why wouldn't I need it, ay?!"

"Cuz you right" my lover's eyes narrow "someone goin' to get hurt."

The man hadn't time to protest as Robin flung him with unapologetic brutality to the other side of the carriage. He pinned him against the window with his forearm as my breath hitched with titillation and wonderment.

"Get-get hurt-?" Says he, snivelling like a damn coward as his oppressor leans, slowly, threateningly, towards him.

"Yeah" Robin growls, running an elegant tongue across those bestial teeth "*really… really… badly.*"

My lover then instantaneously latches onto his neck, holding him still with overbearing strength. The man flails in a pathetic display, gasping, choking on what once kept him alive before the telling, audible snap of tendons and weak flesh. Silence. Our driver is brutalised with no ounce of remorse present in the sadistic carnality of those narrowed eyes.

Within seconds, blood from his victim's jugular spurts profusely over the window and my lover's face - he is usually cleaner with such butchery, but Robin's previous vendetta was taken into consideration for this grizzly end I've no doubt. He kills as though the man were paper, ripping his neck to shreds and, like a wild animal, exposing the muscle for his consumption.

He squeezes his victim's neck with those beastly claws until he rips yet another series of gashes, drawing every ounce of blood as he hungrily sucks the gaping puncture. An impish tongue dances across the clumsy lacerations, lapping eagerly at the e'er oozing redness. The blood that dribbles down his chin makes me shudder from the very implications. He groans, I mirror such with my own arousal wanting nothing more than to kiss that proficient mouth; I wish most profoundly those lips would suck elsewhere.

Once satisfied, Robin pulls away, glancing to me with a wide, bloodied grin. He wipes his mouth, smearing more across his face in the process as if to paint himself for battle.

"So much for bloodshed, darling" I muse "…that was…"

He smirks "that turn you on, eh?"

"Well" I challenge "only *marginally*-"

"Bullshit, Julie, you *love* it when me do that."

Mary shakes her head "Wish you'd stop showing off. You makes a big mess of the carriage."

"Well" he shrugs with a macabre little snicker "it not like he be using it anymore."

Catherine's Diary, 6th October.

As we, at long last, approach our destination, I cannot help but feel guilty for deceiving the poor gentleman. It was I, after all, who thought to do such.

Both Thomas and Humphrey tell me I needed worry however, what we do is for the greater good - I am sure Mr Beg-Chetwynde will understand and forgive us for deceiving him so - even if it *is* a horrible thing to do, what the occult plan should we think too much of morals would be far, far worse. And besides, we never have to see this Barkley again when this ordeal is over.

Later: The grounds themselves were rather spectacular - I'm still rather disappointed we hadn't the time to look around properly. We walked a long driveway to get to the estate, rows of wooden fencing either side which acted as a threshold for the beautiful greenery which carpeted the land.

Thomas linked my arm in his own, gesturing to the mansion in the near distance. He says he should love to live in a place like this with me - I would too, the country is so very beautiful. I suppose equally it would get my dear away from the horrid memories of Isabelle in London - as much as town is our home, I do understand how it grieves my darling Thomas to be surrounded by such vivid memories of her. Perhaps it a mix of the cool evening air, but in that moment a shudder jolts through me.

I cannot dwell on that at present however, Mr Bone calls to us from further up the driveway.

"Here!" Says he, pointing to a stretch of field beyond the trees "I think this is it!"

"Are you certain?" My husband asks.

Mr Bone nods "quite. Look at the formation, there's nothing else like it around. Sticks out like a sore thumb."

"Well" I opine "I suppose we ought to... *investigate*?"

My husband chuckles "indeed, madam historian! Please, after you."

He opens the gate for myself and Mr Bone, and we begin the walk to the obscure circle of stones. The journey did not take long as most was downhill, the stones were situated in a valley where the hilly landscape joins. The house was on the highest behind us which unnerved me momentarily as it reminded me of a guard or watchman; I couldn't help but question whether Mr Beg-Chetwynde had really gone away at all.

Mr Bone was a few paces behind as he carried the bag full of tools, but he soon joined us at the site. I must admit, on first inspection the stones appeared rather insignificant for a supposed ritual - them being so dull and covered in moss didn't seem fitting at all; as though we'd fallen victim to some terrible anticlimax. Upon closer examination however, the stones were littered with queer inscriptions that made me believe there was more to them, something far grander than first anticipated.

"Well, here we are" states Mr Bone with sudden emotion "…we made it."

"Indeed we have" says Thomas "to think, everything we've done - you've done - has all lead to this moment, the final puzzle piece, so to speak."

"Ah, well, I couldn't have done it without you Thorne," he then turns to me "and your lady here. We make quite the team."

"After all this it's… it's finally over" my dear shakes his head "seems rather odd, don't you think? To end in such a way?"

"Well, it's not entirely over with. But I get your point, almost seems too easy."

I chuckle "lest you forget how much we've all been through. I'd hardly call it *easy.*"

"Aye miss, hammering some stones will be a blessing in comparison."

"Well then," My Husband takes a chisel from the bag, tossing the other to Mr Bone " we best get on with it."

The men make quick work of gauging the stones, Mr Bone concluded a break would suffice as opposed to absolute destruction (something about bindings being broken? I'm not sure I quite understand, but of course would never dispute it with him.)

Thomas makes the first crack, the old stones crumble relatively easily under his chisel. Humphrey assists With a determined expression but I suppose his demeanour is oft' serious. Heaven knows what he must've been put through before my Thomas arrived. I do understand his manner, one supposes it would be awfully foolish to let your guard down at the last hurdle.

My attention slowly diminishes as they continue, the evening draws nearer with every break until only one, the largest stone in the centre, remains.

"Last one" pants Mr Bone, wiping sweat from his brow "at last."

The phrase rings in my head as I take to looking at the scenery, I find myself, in that moment, awash with prosperity and relief. For, he's right. All that we've been through has amounted to this moment, and I felt so terribly fortunate to experience the end. And thus I look to the setting sun o'er the mountainous horizons, one final peak of light before the glow of the full moon replaces it. But, O' heavens how terribly naive I was for all these assumptions! It is then I pause, moving to clutch my Husband's arm before he hammers - I spy something that throws a great spanner in the works.

"What, my darling?" He turns to me "is something the matter?"

"T-Tomas... *look...*"

Three figures appear at the end of my finger, and begin to descend towards us.

IX

Upon Catherine's exclamation of terror, I turn to where she anxiously points. As sure as her word three figures, like shadowless spirits, walk down the hill towards us. Even with the moon behind them I could not make out their faces, but I of course knew instantly who they were.

"It appears we've company" says Thomas, instinctively clutching his Wife's arm "too easy, you say?"

"Aye, I take it back Thorne. I take it *all* back."

In that moment, I felt positively trapped - as though they were surveying our helplessness from above before descending on their easy prey. The bowl-like valley rendered us as advantaged as sitting ducks. Instinctively I reach for my bag, drawing from it the stakes I'd hoped the Lord would've insured us never to use. Catherine blanches quite profoundly as I hand one to her; she clasps the unlikely weapon in trembling fingers. I then turn to Thomas, who's countenance appears almost apologetic.

"Shouldn't we wait?" Says he with pitiful naivety "perhaps one could solve this with diplomacy?"

"Oh, Thomas" I shake my head, handing him the only means of meaningful affliction "these vampires shan't cooperate. You know that."

"But-"

"Thorne" I look him sternly in the eyes "you and I both know it's kill or be killed."

I anticipated further protest, but instead the man merely nods, accepting the wooden stake with a wash of anger that creases his his youthful visage. Whether it be the divine will of God to live, or the determination to protect his wife, the poet appeared ready for battle.

Damn good job, mind, for the occult draw e're closer as the three of us exhale. Wordlessly, as if automated, we form a line - the frontline.

"Oh, goodness where's father?" Catherine laments "should he not be here by now?"

"Please, madam think not of him" I urge "we can handle this ourselves."

Finally, the two sides meet - like heaven and hell, good and evil we stand before one another with expressions of both solemnity and rage. I cannot suppress a shudder at the thought of what is to come, but for the sake of my companions I stand my ground.

"So" I say, my weapon tightly enclosed in my fist "…here we are at last."

"It's been too long Humph," Julian facades a grin, but one cannot mistake the hostility that creeps into his tone "after your little friends burned our boat and all, I was starting to think you didn't like us."

"Noticed you done' the stones too" Robin gestures "left us one, though. Maybe still wants to fuck us after all?"

His obscene response makes my blood boil "shut your mouth! This isn't a fucking *game*!"

"Is for us, sweetheart," Julian muses before turning to Mrs Thorne with an unmistakably libidinous expression "…and who might this be?"

Thomas turns to his wife "behind me, Catherine. You're not to trust this imp."

"Aye, these bastards should have their bestial hands all over you" I shake my head, spitting words with purposeful venom "this is no place for a woman like yourself madam. I urge thee. Stand back."

"Oh?" Says Mary folding her arms "What that makes me then?"

"Ignore him" their damnable ringleader grunts "so eh, we doin' this easy way or hard way?"

"We're not backing down for anything" I assert "I suggest you disband your filthy cult before someone gets hurt. You're not to continue with this depraved, bloody scheme, you understand?"

The vampire grins, a horrid bloody grin, before cracking his neck. He looks to me with piercing blue eyes and an expression of sadistic amusement.

"Mmh" says he "I was hoping for the hard way."

The calmness of his visage does unease me, for one cannot help but think their indifference comes from holding the indisputable upper hand. I know of their powers, but I know equally of our strength. If the frontline was a hundred men, so be it. If the frontline were two and a woman, thus be it too. I do remember longing for the miraculous appearance of Patrick and the Captain. Perhaps then we would not look so vexingly vulnerable.

"... So be it," I say, in the straightest tone my nerves can muster.

Julian looks to the stake in my right hand "you really want to do this? Just let us get on, Humphrey, you don't know what you're dealing with."

Their cockiness only spurs me on, rage welling up inside me to an extent I knew not myself capable of. My brows furrow, looking to those hellish beings with a profound loathing.

"As God as my witness, we *shall* be victorious."

"Oh, Humphrey," Robin tuts, walking towards me until he stands uncomfortably close "there is no God. But if there were… it'd be *me*."

His gravelly words send shivers down my spine, but I fight to facade confidence. His tactics are merely to intimidate and I cannot afford to fall for them. There is simply too much weighting on our success.

I know not the point our fight commenced, lost in my own thoughts I merely look to the teeth that protrude from our enemies mouths - pupils dilating as if aroused by the prospect of bloodshed. I'm on guard, yet before I know it I'm on the ground. Robin pounces upon me with all his carnal strength, pinning my wrist so that my weapon cannot be utilised. Thomas protects the final stone in the corner of my vision, but I know not where Julian went - I hadn't time to dwell on it either, for my ears are pierced with a terrible cry - Catherine, it is her's unmistakably.

Amongst my futile struggles I watch as Mary holds Mrs Thorne against a tree, pinning her against it with horrid brutality. The poor girl screams, yet both myself and Thomas cannot overpower the impossible strength of the occult.

"You leave her alone!" Thomas shouts with a sudden surge of fury "off her, witch! You'll have her when I'm dead!"

I cannot bear to watch as she continues to scream, nor can I listen to her husband's desperate sobs. It is for that reason that I initially fail to spot the two figures that creep towards her - instead, I find myself startled by some great shout. I'm hit across the face, but through blurred vision and ringing ears I mark the unmistakable silhouettes of Patrick and the Captain.

My memory is hazy, I know not how they did it, but upon my second glance the woman is tackled down by paternal wrath. Despite the circumstance, I feel a victorious smile tug at my lips as Patrick sees to the affrighted Catherine.

Of course, all is not over, for the woman fights remorselessly against the Captain's grasp, clawing at his arms in desperate anger.

"Stake her heart!" I call "you've the chance! Do it!"

"I shan't kill a woman-" The Captain visibly shakes at the prospect, the being before him writhing uncontrollably in aid of escaping his grasp "Sir, I cannot!"

I know not how righteous it is for one to scream 'kill, kill it goddamn you!' But the situation swayed nought from thus: Kill or be killed; for in that moment we were in some primal battle of death and profane distraction, gorilla warfare of the most bestial quality. Weaponry enclosed in trembling hands we bore our bare souls for penance, our enemy before us solely to be eradicated.

"That is no woman, Captain!" I plead, shouting across the makeshift battlefield "you must! In God's name you must, for Catherine, damn you!"

His visage noticeably shifts as I utter his daughter's name; like Stanley at Bosworth field his duality ceased in aid of supporting victory. With all his paternal might he henceforth cries out in anguish, ramming that lethal weapon remorselessly into the woman's chest. I know not if the others saw for i was preoccupied with watching Patrick pull the affrighted Catherine to her feet.

The Captain repeats the motion with vindictive anger; Mrs Thorne buries her face into his shoulder with a sob. I must admit that I could not suppress my own discomfort as the creature writhed, hissed, underneath him - I forget that the occult are capable of should we let them walk free.

Before I could dwell on it further, she ceases her struggle. The Captain stands with a freshly bloodied shirt, looking to them both in turn with a grave expression. Within moments, Catherine is in his arms; she heaves great sobs into his chest as the shaken man gently pats her hair. I know not of his true emotion - I merely watched the scene from the corner of my eye as I continue to fight against Robin's grasp, kicking at his chest that was seemingly made of stone. I only wish I could've been more present in the sentiment.

"You-you came" says she, looking to him with teary eyes "father I thought you were-"

"Shh, shh, Kitty. I'm here now-"

Suddenly, the pair turn to look across the field. Catherine's eyes widen as our separate battles instantaneously blur. She gasps, clutching her father's arm as he clasps his bloodied weapon.

"Oh, oh father!" She urges "you *must* help them!"

"Stay here-" says he sternly, before running towards me.

His figure approaches - somewhere, a cry of agony - and then I remember no more.

Catherine Thorne's Diary, 6th October.

I do not wish to write. Diaries act as written memories after all, but how should I forget what happened? I shan't wish to ever look back on this horrid book, the only reason I pick up my pen once more is to document this supernatural ordeal. Perhaps in time someone, should they believe me, will take my warning.

I could not suppress tears as my father left me once more, worried for him, Mr bone - and my husband. I did as he instructed waiting by the tree, for a while, but eventually I moved to another for I could not bear the sight of that poor girl. In that moment, I could not shake the feeling that perhaps it should be me lying there - the woman was stronger and faster than I. Yet now she lies bloodied with a gaping hole in her chest, her exposed heart now still like her expressionless visage. What would've become of it if my father hadn't have intervened? As I survey the battlefield through misty eyes I wonder what God really meant for us, and so I quietly pray - for then I've an excuse to close my eyes.

To the faceless woman, my foe of whom I never met nor knew your name. May the Lord now take you, and your restless soul be still. May you find peace and be forgiven from a world that lead you astray.

I then exhale, starting a few words for my husband before being jarred back by some horrific cries - both of pain, yet different voices. Through my fingers I look up, yet remove them hastily for I believe my eyes deceive me.

Thomas must've escaped the occults grasp for he now held the blonde man down against the stone we hadn't yet destroyed. With an expression of fury, or personal vendetta I know not how he acquired, my husband draws a bloody stake from his chest. He steps back, wiping his brow, and I hadn't even the time to feel.

From elsewhere, I hear a shout, and look to where the other vampire balls his fists. His expression is something I cannot place either - neither did I have the time, great heavens! With the strength of an animal he, in a fit of rage, threw Mr Bone as though he were a lifeless doll. The man must've landed ten feet away, brutality hitting his back against the stone wreckage. I gasp, hands over my mouth in petrified astonishment. Mr Butcher rushes to his aid, and I feel so hopelessly useless that I did not think to do the same. For there I was, paralysed with fear whilst the men risked their lives.

Thus I rose to my feet, misty eyed yet determined, and ran to his aid. In front of me, the vampire runs impossibility fast toward Thomas and where the Captain has joined him. Knowing I cannot catch him, I call desperately to my loved ones.

"Thomas! Father!" I cry, in the loudest voice my sobs permit "look out!"

As if on instinct they reach for their weapons as this vampire rushes e're closer. He growls, flaming-eyed and wild like that of a lion or tiger.

"Please-" I pant, "don't hurt t-"

And then he runs past them both, for they were never his target.

In some unseen turn of events the beast, with haste, reaches the stone. Complete indifferent to his surroundings, as thought the battle meant nothing. With new found vulnerability he looks over the dying man before lifting him gently, cradling him close to his chest. The blonde winces in discomfort as the three of us look on in astonishment - for I do believe a tear rolled down the other's cheek.

"Shh, n-no, come on Julian-" says the vampire with a desperate smile "you're alright, is ok-you be fine- you *fine*-"

"Robin-" says Julian, before coughing blood on the back of his hand "I-I don't think I am-"

"You *are*- I won't let you go-" the man insists, a slight tremor to his voice as he holds the blonde tighter as he drifts in and out of consciousness "hey? Hey- please, your gunna' be fine- promise-j-just *stay*-p-please don't go-"

"*Robbie*-"

He shakes his head as tears roll down his cheeks "Can't lose you, can't lose you Julie *please*-!"

Julian gives a tired snicker, choking slightly on the blood that fills his lungs before coughing more up in a brave attempt to smile "I-I think you might have to, baby..."

"N-*no* it-"

"...You're allowed to say 'I told you so'."

He sniffs, holding the man's face with a fond expression "You s-such an idiot, y-you know that?... even now."

"Yeah, well" Julian coughs, wincing as Robin caresses his pale face " I r-recon this idiot has to go now."

"Y-you *don't*- no, no-" he shakes his head, voice unusually high and cracking "please Julie, don't go, don't go-!"

"Hey, hey you'll-" he hisses in pain, extraordinary still facading a smile "you'll be fine, you're so strong Robbie, so strong-"

"N-not without you-" he shakes "I can't- you're my everything, *please*-"

There is silence for a while, an eerie, poignant tranquility where nobody dared utter a word.

"...Robin?" Julian's voice was so faint, so strained I could not hear what he then said, but from the other's tears and the pressing of foreheads I do believe it were '*I love you.*'

Julian clutches his shoulder as they kiss - really, I do not know why I didn't expect such. I watch curiously as they continue, lips firmly pressed together all the while smearing blood over their mouths but in a manner so desperately romantic I didn't think it at all grotesque. They close their eyes as tears freely fall - both holding so tightly as if to never let the other go.
Inevitably, Julian's hand falls limp, and Robin sets him down on the stone.

I cannot suppress my own tear as the broken man falls to his knees, balling his fists in anger before letting out a loud cry to the heavens that sounded more like a wolf's howl. In anguish he buries his face in his hands, sobs muffled in his palms as the once invincible vampire crumbles. In that moment I thought it horridly selfish to have ever rejoiced over my husband being alive, for another lover is dead. They feel as profoundly as you or I - that bare, human emotion that cannot be misinterpreted. That is how I would feel, should Thomas lay on that stone. The only thing that separates us and the occult was killing - yet now we have done the same. Indeed, as the man looked upon the other, I knew we were scarcely different after all.

"… I love you too, Julian" he shakes, before kissing his lips once more "… you with the stars now."

The man then turns to address us, yet by this point I have realised this matter had distracted me form my original task. With a gasp I look to Mr Bone - he does not look well at all. With haste therefore I rip a piece of my dress before tossing it to Mr Butcher. He graciously accepts such, wrapping it firmly around the man's bleeding head.

"You'll be alright, Humphrey-" Patrick reassures "just hold on-"

"Oh, so he get to live, eh?!" Robin angrily shouts, with such malicious volume we all simultaneously jump "he allowed to live?! Why?! What make *him* so fucking special?!"

"We had to put an end to this!" My father calls back "you murderous fiends, we shan't let you continue-"

The vampire furiously wipes a tear from his eye "You no different from me! You kill everyone I care about! J-ulian, M-" he looks to where the woman lies in the field, he must've loved her too for he looks away with a pained expression "*Mary*. You kill' em all! Yet you still, *still* call yourselves righteous?! Your type always so entitle, so superior! Thing just cuz' this God tell you one thing, must eradicate *everything* that acts otherwise! How righteous is genocide, eh?! Tell me that!"

"It's for the greater good" Thomas justifies, clutching my arm tightly as the man approaches "you've enslaved, assaulted, *killed*- don't you see? You wish to expand your cultish ways, turn everyone in society because deep down you know - know if not forced our type could never co-exist!"

Robin halts, and for a moment I know not what he is thinking. I expect the worst - in a fit of hellish rage for him to destroy us all

- but instead he exhales, looking to us both defeated and profoundly tired.

"… you win" says he at last "me just a cog in our order. I couldn't do it, they send another to-"

I hadn't the time to dwell on his words, for out of nowhere a stake appears through his chest from behind, the brutality of the impact causing blood to instantaneously spurt from his mouth. He glances down, pawing at the affliction evidently as confused as I, before falling lifelessly to the floor. I gasp, clutching my husband as my father instinctively reaches for my hand.

From the meagre light the moon provided, I can just make out the shadow that caused such. Holding the bloodied weapon, it steps over the body towards us. The figure wears a red cloak with a veil covering their face. They give a small kick to Robin's side "…expendable indeed."

"W-who *are* you?!" My father demands "answer me!"

"I would've thought *one* of you would've recognised me."

Slowly, they cast the veil from their face. My father and myself glance to each other with blank expressions, both futility hoping the other would provide an answer. I then look to Thomas, but he is not as I expect. My husband's countenance had shifted quite profoundly - as white as a sheet with an open moth of utter disbelief.

"… I- *Isabelle*?"

"Did you miss me, Thomas?"

Thomas Thorne's Diary, 6/7th October.

Everything blurred at her implausible confirmation, my wife's words drowned out by some horrid ringing in my ear. Through blurred vision I could see her - as lovely and vibrant as she ever was - yet that was not her stood before me. It couldn't be. I felt faint at the very prospect, leaning onto my father-in-law for support as he tried with all his might to keep me standing. I must be dreaming, or indeed dead. Why else should my dead wife be stood before me like some voluptuous angel?

"I-it can't be" I finally splutter, yet it is she in all her youthful splendour "It can't-"

"Oh, but it *is*, my darling" her voice like enchanting silk and honey "*your* Isabelle."

"B-but how?" With trepidation I step forward, shaking my foggy head "this is impossible! I'm dreaming!"

"Indeed, I am a dream to you Tom, yet very real."

"Y- you *died*-" I insist, tears brimming in my eyes as she begins a sultry walk towards me "T-the accident- I watched them lower you into the damn ground-"

"The Police never told you what *sort* of accident, did they? Left my punctured body on the autopsy table - I was gone before the mortician could decipher anything."

" N-*no*-" she places a hand to my trembling face "It- it was a *carriage*- they wouldn't let me see you because it disfigured- I saw your *casket*-"

"*Empty* casket, Tom" her red lips so close to mine as she emits a sadistic little snicker "you buried an empty box."

"No-no!" I struggle, but her air was so hopelessly intoxicating I could not help but yield to her seduction "I-*Isabelle*-"

"Leave him alone!" Catherine pleads through tears, I believe she would've stormed over if her father had not prohibited it "he's not yours anymore!"

"Oh, but he never *was* yours" says she in a breathy whisper "you never stopped thinking about me, did you Thomas?"

"P-please" I choke "I couldn't-"

"Join me" Isabelle requests at last "leave this life that's been making you so miserable. We'll start anew, us two shall rule the vampire order - you'd do that for me, wouldn't you?"

"Thomas!" I head my wife call from behind me "please, you mustn't!"

I turn my head to look, but Isabelle promptly pulls me back to my eyes. She smiles, that irresistible smile, before I see those green eyes I once did with Julian.

"Oh, Isabelle" she leans in closer as I exhale "… our time together ended many moons ago."

I do not grant her time to struggle as I ram the wooden stake into her chest, the vampire that was once my wife hisses and flails - and then I knew such a beast could never be my Isabelle. At long last she falls to the ground, her expression restful and calm like I always imagined. Catherine runs to me as I embrace her, for my place has always been with her.

"Oh-Thomas-" she sobs "you-you-"

"It is you I love, Catherine. Perhaps I did love her once, but she who lays before us is not that same woman."

"I love you, Thomas" says she through teary eyes. I lean in for a kiss, but we are interrupted by Patrick's shout.

"Help!" He calls with urgency "please, we need to get Mr Bone out of here!"

We rush over to where the pale man lies, his half-lidded eyes focused on the sky as he slurs some unintelligible words.

"It's alright Humphrey-" I annunciate "we'll get you help-"

"T-tell Sophie I love her, would you?" He whispers.

"There's nowt for miles" Mr Butcher laments "we'll-we'll have to carry him-"

"there's no need for that" I assure him "you'll tell her yourself-"

"As it will be" asserts Catherine's father "hang in there, young man."

I watch his stained eyes close as the Captain lifts him from the ground.

X (EPILOGUE)

<u>Thomas Thorne's Diary, 31st October.</u>

To whomever should be unfortunate enough to read these dammed pages, you must forgive me for not writing. From whenever my last entry was penned, my party have spent the time recovering - though a full return to normality would surly be impossible. Physically we are well, but our minds shall forever be tainted by our collective experiences.

This, after all, shall be my final entry. Nothing further should e're be said on the horrors that have afflicted us over these weeks - yet for my own comfort one feels obligated to conclude such with where this ordeal has taken us respectively. Of course, as a writer I shall surly pick up a pen once more - but never for the likes of this loathsome Diary.

Catherine's father was able to signal help upon the main road adjacent the Barkley estate - by some miracle a lone carriage headed to the Binat town took Humphrey free of charge to the nearest hospital. Patrick n'er took his eyes off the man throughout the entirety of the journey whilst I kept my own focused on my Wife. We neither of us spoke, of course, instead our hands clamped together like vices as the Captain's anxious words faded into that of incomprehensible murmurs. Through all the traumatised silence there was one thought that never left my mind - amongst all that occurred, that is. I couldn't help but wonder if the carriage were some-sort of divine apology; it were as if amongst the visceral affliction and pain the Lord had decided that no more should perish tonight. I look over to the pale Mr Bone, and thought him very lucky indeed.

We arrived soon after, told to seek refuge in the hotel in town as there was nothing more we could do at present. In all our aching tiredness we accepted, with the wholehearted promise to Humphrey that we should send a telegram to a Miss Sophie with her address disclosed in a weak murmur.

"You won't here anything back… we haven't spoken in a while" said he with a pained sigh "but I'd like to anyway, all things considered."

"Of course, Humphrey. But for now you must rest."

"Don't say that, Tom-" he laughs before coughing "I might not wake up."

I am certain none of our party got an ounce of sleep that night.

It must've been four our five days before our return to the hospital. Apart from the thick bandages around the man's head, he looked in far greater spirits. Humphrey smiled upon our arrival, asking after ourselves and Sophie - to which, regrettably, we hadn't heard a word. Patrick assured him her word would take a while from Transylvania, but from the man's face I could tell he saw clean through his pitiful optimism. At a time like this, I couldn't imagine Catherine being anywhere by my side, and thus I do believe I understood his anguish. It would be a lie if I opined I did not still mourn for Isabelle.

We kept Humphrey comfortable that afternoon, The Captain told tales of his own injury in the Crimea. I, of course, read poetry Inspired from our time together. In that moment, queer as it sounds, I felt no feeling of loss or sorrow as opposed to inexplicable warmth. As though, amongst the hardship, I had formed a priceless bond with people I fondly consider family. We jest, we smile; amongst the darkness we've created a fire - our flames e're growing with laughter and jovial defiance.

I know not when, perhaps hours later, my anecdote was interrupted by a commotion outside the ward. I could not see the figures involved - merely voices and shadows in the corridor.

"Mon amour, où est-il!?" Demands a woman - French, if I am not mistaken "where is my Humphrey? Réponds-moi!"

"You cannot just enter, madam" says one of the nurses, clearly rather agitated "you will disturb the patients-it's-"

"Just *une* minute, si vous plait" she urges "please, I *must* see him!"

Instantaneously she marches through the door, eyes surveying the ward before her harsh exterior crumbles. She rushes towards us - my telegram in hand with teary eyes.

"...*Sophie*?" the man's eyes widen "you're here-? I thought you-"

"Tu Crétin!" the woman scolds "I thought you were *dead*!"

He deadpans "...Charming."

I watch with a smile as she shakes her head, crouching by his side as she takes Humphrey's hand.

"I... did not think I'd ever see you again" she lets their fingers entwine "after we... argumenté... je pensais que c'était fini. You had... moved on."

"Oh, Soph - I never stopped thinking about you" Humphrey looks to her in all honesty "you know I only took that job because of *you*."

"Y-you never came back. Humphrey, I... did not think you had survived it."

"I tried, darling I *tried* to escape-" he then looks to me thankfully "If it wasn't for Thomas here I might not have."

"Merci, Thomas" Sophie grants me a small smile "*thank you*."

It is a simple exhibition of gratitude, yet her visage yields great profundity.

I nod "your husband is a good man."

The woman smiles, and I believe she was to say something more, but she instead turns to Humphrey with sudden urgency.

"Oh but, Humphrey!" Says she "your head, what happened? Ça a l'air douloureux!"

"It's a long story, my love" the man replies "not for now. It only matters that you're here."

"Désolé, Humphrey" she sighs "I am sorry. I should not have made you-"

"It's In the past Sophie, I shan't think any more of it" he tries a smile before pointing to his neck "besides, they're going down. Not quite as red as before, I recon."

"Oh, Humphrey, mon amour, you poor-"

"I-I'm sorry" Patrick suddenly opines, shaking his head "y-you knew about the-?"

"She knew all about the vampires, aye" Humphrey replies, as if the information of no value "met me after she moved over from France - we kept having spats over whether they were real or not. All came to a head one day so I said 'I'll get a job at that place, alright? Do some investigation and- well, you know first hand how well that went."

"T-the research, the books-" I stutter "those were-?"

"Moi" Sophie shrugs indifferently "you don't seriously think this, this *homme sans cervelle* read all those books himself did you?"

"Hey!" Humphrey protests, although I am yet to translate what was so offensive "perhaps you're the brains, but I'm most certainly the braun. These bandages show *my* bloody sacrifice."

"You men and your muscles" Her demeanour then noticeably shifts "but I am…sorry. I should've been there-"

"Well" Patrick laughs dryly as if to lighten the mood "we certainly could have done with your expertise a few weeks ago-"

She rolls her eyes "nearly got yourselves killed without me, did you?"

"A-ah on the contrary, young lady - we utilised a variety of highly effective strategies, all risking our damn *lives* to-"

Patrick places a hand on his shoulder "she's joking. She didn't mean it like that."

"She didn't-? Ah-" He looks at him before nodding to Sophie "my apologies, madam."

Intelligent eyes survey the pair before she whispers to Humphrey. I know not quite what she said, nor the means to do her translation justice, but it went something along the lines of:

"your friends do they … how do you…. *chauve-souris pour l'autre équipe*?"

"Please! Only batsman I know to be scared of balls."

He laughs before she does the same. A kiss to his forehead tells me perhaps we are now intruding on their reunion. Wordlessly therefore, I stand, nodding to my party as I begin to exit.

"May you recover soon, Humphrey" my wife nods upon our departure.

"I shall never forget what we've accomplished" says Humphrey "what you've done for me, all of you, I shan't ever have the means to repay you."

"Our lives shall suffice" I reply "let us think no more of the past - I've had my fair share of such. You shall write to me instead in the future with all your wonderful happenings."

"And so it shall be, Thorne. *Thank you.*"

****

And thus we find ourselves in present times, Our party have returned to London and continue to reside in familiar streets. The poetry I wrote in Transylvania has been sold to Macmillan. Inc to which my macabre writings are readily being sold throughout London. With this new income, I've the hope to move Catherine and myself to a larger estate in the country. As her name is mentioned, I must opine she handles the new adjustments miraculously well - her positivity has not been tainted by the events and she remains, as ever, my beacon of light.

She informs me that Dr Cooper has since written to her regarding Alison's health - the girl has made significant progress in her recovery and will soon return to London. My wife looks forward to reuniting, and I do suppose such friendship will further us towards normality. Perhaps one thinks it queer to opine, but it appears our stopping of the occult has broken the spell of her madness - as though the two were inexplicable linked. I know not how, of course, but the stopping of one chaos appears to have solved the other. Believe it not, all you skeptics, but there is equal possibility she was always well - the phrase 'method in her madness' springs to mind as I recall her encrypted prose. I hesitate to dwell on the unusual- indeed, within these pages I have detailed my fair share of such. If one thing can be taken from my witness it is to fear the supernatural - not those who rave its truth. I am merely elated Catherine should have company once more whilst I write. Assurance be to all those who read my works - our future yields prosperity as time forever distances us from our troubled past.

In other revelations (I know not of detail) my wife's letters of enquiry have demonstrated her father is similarly coping - he resides now with Mr Butcher in a cottage in the seaside town of Weymouth to which they oft' take walks along the Beach. I am informed our artillery is yet to be destroyed, instead is kept as queer decoration within the living room as an ode to our daring adventures. I myself think it rather strange to keep such a bloody souvenir, but I suppose it can only be celebrated that it is none of our own that adorns those wooden stakes. Catherine, and therefore myself also, believe them to be content with the new arrangements as they certainly seem to enjoy each-other's company. One cannot comment further on the matter (alas should these words e're be published) but one can only hope their retirement shall be best spent in the prosperous rays of sun. The strengthened bonds and recognition of family during these past few months will ensure I visit often - it should be fitting to, like the swallow, migrate to warmer climate.

In final news, a letter from Humphrey informs me he has made a full recovery, himself and Sophie have since moved back to Transylvania with the hope of continuing their research. I am told he is thinking of publishing his diary as a work of non-fiction, to perhaps warn the public of what we faced and urges me to do the same. For now, I am undecided - if I were to do so I would, of course, have to make… edits. I am not certain how I feel about capitalising off our hardship, but then again it is our own and we have the moral right to do so! I suppose if I correlated our respective entries it could warrant valuable perspectives - perhaps I think too economically, but that should surly make for an enticing read (one that would make a larger demographic aware of the danger, of course. This book should be nothing but a cautionary tale.)

Regardless of what becomes of it, I must conclusively opine that whether the contents of this diary are deemed a historic breakthrough or warrants a great vendetta against our society's status quo (one is inclined to think the latter, indeed, who should believe the likes of a deranged bohemian?) I must urge thee to not dismiss what resides beyond the veil as I once did - thankful only that those I love should survive my error. All that I have witnessed have sealed my fate as forever tormented by such a troubling ordeal- scarred yes; but I suppose we're equally wiser for it. All those who have died shall be remembered hereafter for proof that one can be victorious, yet I have learned that perhaps evil is not so much black or white as technicolored. Think me a fool for believing our enemy capable of feelings beyond concentrated malice, but it is this depth that renders them so terribly, deceptively human. Do not forget threat of those invisible to convention - they grow closer with every dismissal. For when evil shall rise again (as I oft' fear) I trust thee to protect our women, our children. Never again shalt London face threats from their type so long as we open our eyes to the possibility of the impossible.

Heed this warning, good friends.
Adieu,

Thomas Thorne.

Acknowledgments

With thanks to everyone who enjoys and reads my work, I've appreciated all the support very much.

Robin Pearson 2023

Printed in Great Britain
by Amazon